flirty thirty

A NERDY THIRTIES NOVEL

Maya and Cooper's Story

CASSIE MAE

Dedicated to those who found gray hairs long before they were ready for them. Solidarity, my friends.

1

Kiss and Ditch

"On this day, my thirtieth birthday, I propose that every Sunday starting now will be Naked Day. All in favor?"

I set down my steaming cup of coffee, topped with my traditional birthday whipped cream and chocolate shavings, and raise my right hand to the square. Tom and Kat sit with their legs poised in the air as they continue to lick their privates.

"It's unanimous!" I grin, placing my hand back on my mug. "I hereby declare this the first official Naked Sunday."

Tom yawns, finds the sun beam that's strewn across my brand new area rug, and immediately crashes into his day time sleep. Kat sniffs the air, just now noticing the aroma of my morning treat. I'd let her lick the bottom of the mug, but the last time that happened she tore up my bed canopy trying to mimic Jackie Chan.

Since my cats are my only roommates, I allow myself a tiny jump in celebration, my loosey goosey larger-than-average chest nearly knocking me over without the brazierial support. How positively *freeing* that feels. I let a smile tilt up on my face as I take my mug and walk buck-A naked to the plush chair I keep in front of my 70-inch.

There are moments in life that you just know you've got it good. This is my moment. Thirty years old, single, living in a house I own with things that are all mine, no kids to watch me walk around naked, looking out for number one and enjoying the peace that comes with living alone. Nobody close to me understands just how perfect the scenario is.

My phone rings on my bare thigh as I scroll through my recorded Ellens, and I hit pause to glance at the number. Ah… case in point. My sister has sent me a birthday message along with a picture of a guy who knows her husband's co-worker's aunt, and she just knows we are *meant to be!* She's ready to set me up with him for this weekend.

Dating I can do. Sex I can do. Fun, fun, all good. But I am not ready to strap my chain to someone else's ball for the rest of my life. Having seen the result of falling in love up close from not only my sister and brother-in-law, but my brother and his wife, my best friend and her husband, and my partner and her husband, and their combined total of nine kids (and one on the way) of whom I've all babysat for, I'm quite content on spending my days alone with Tom and Kat, sitting naked and binge watching the newest Netflix craze.

I quickly tap the picture to make it bigger and tilt my head to the side, considering. It's been a couple months since I've done a one-on-one, and he's not too bad to look at. Kind eyes, good smile, strong chin, little round in the middle, but I've always kind-of liked that. I snap a selfie with a squishy, funny face and send it back to her with a

"Thanks!" and a "Let's go for it!" If anything, it'll get her off my back for a couple of weeks.

She chimes back with, *Are you naked???* And I laugh and tell her, *It's my birthday! I'm dressing accordingly. ;)* When I don't hear another chime right away, I hit play and watch Ellen, drink coffee, and plan out what other things I should do while in my birthday suit. I bet baking would be more fun without the worry of flour getting on any clothing. Cookies will be made today.

Kat nuzzles up against the back of my hand, and I grant her request and rub her butt as she turns and sticks her tail in the air. I've only had her for five months, but I already know what spots she doesn't want scratched. The faded claw marks over my wrists prove my failed attempts at cuddling.

Tom's my lazier roommate—granted he is nearing his fifties in cat years—so I usually get my cuddle time with him. Between the two of them and my giant family, I get all the company I could ever want or need. So I don't think I'll be meeting the future Mr. Maya Baker this weekend, no matter how much my sister wants it for me.

A commercial comes on for the some kind of cologne— one that puts a spotlight on a set of gorgeous blue eyes and a sharp jawline, and I let out a gurgled "Oh" around my coffee and whipped cream and hoist up from the chair. It's almost "Handsome Man-o'clock." Every morning a Grecian God jogs down my street, sweating and smiling and looking very much available. While I may not be looking for a permanent companion, I am definitely up for a bit of innocent flirting. A few weeks ago, he waved at me while I was trimming my rosebushes. Just the other day he said, "Good morning," followed by a delicious grin that had me fantasizing all through my morning appointments.

Today, I think I'd like to say more than two words to him. It'll be my birthday gift to me.

Sighing at the fact that I will have to put *something* on to go outside on the first established Naked Sunday, I slip my arms into a ragged and worn hoodie that's so large that it falls about mid-thigh. It belonged to an old boyfriend who, like all those who came before him, showed his true colors after only a few months of dating. Our relationship fell victim to what I've dubbed the Bore of More. The truth is, after the honeymoon stage, things got boring. There wasn't much more to what we had outside of sex, and even that started to lose its appeal when there was no mystery around it.

But his clothes were very comfortable, and after a mutual breakup, he was nice enough to let me keep something from the Big and Tall store he shopped at.

I stuff my feet into a pair of slippers my mom uses when she stays over—the woman is never warm enough—and walk out with my hot coffee, a little nervous at the draft around my butt since I may be showing cheek. I reach around and hold the material down, doing a very sexy waddle to my patio chair in the corner of my porch.

My neighborhood is basically on the side of a mountain, my front door facing the valley below. The sun's coming up behind me, casting a yellow glow on my lawn as the dew shines back at me. I probably could've come outside naked and no one would know—Sunday mornings are quiet and with my nearest neighbor quite a few acres away, there would be no one to call the cops with a lewd complaint. But since I know the beach blond jogging man is coming, I make sure that I'm efficiently covered as my eyes fall to my mailbox.

"Oh!" I say, my drink spilling off the sides of the mug and splashing to the cement under me. I forgot to grab the mail yesterday, and I'm positive there's a check in there. Oma always sends me a check for my birthday, but she's starting to lose it so I get four a year: one for every month ending in "Y." I only cash the real one for myself. The rest go to my brother Jim and his wife Katie because they've got more mouths to feed and less change to do it with.

I bring my coffee to my lips as I make my way down my walk and dig through the mailbox, the whipped cream creating a mustache that I swipe away with the back of my hand. Junk mail, junk, junk… thank heavens I went to paperless billing because I'm almost positive those would be next. No card from Oma yet.

The mailbox flumps as I close it back up and stretch. I've always loved being a Spring baby. Nine times out of ten I get a breezy 70 degrees and a great view from my front porch to greet the day. You know, before I spend it in front of the TV.

I take a great big inhale and soak up the mountain morning scent before I go in and celebrate in my own naked way, and as the deep breath leaves my slightly parted mouth, I catch my morning jogger heading down my street.

Speaking of great views and Spring weather, hello abdominal muscles. Haven't seen those in a long while. Winter doesn't exactly boast its appeal for shirtless runners, my dating record hasn't included many cut and fit men— not complaining, of course; I enjoy men of all sizes—and my own muscles are hidden under about ten pounds of pooch.

Happy birthday, indeed. I'm not one to deprive themselves of free eye candy, so I casually pretend to take in the morning view and sip on my chocolaty treat as he gets closer and closer.

I wonder for the millionth time where he lives. While this neighborhood boasts itself on privacy, most of us know who lives where, but there are new plots available a few blocks on the upper side of the mountain. I've been selling them off to clients I feel like I can enjoy as neighbors. But from the moment he arrived a month ago, jogging and gleaming down my street, my curiosity has gotten the better of me on more than one occasion.

He's close now, close enough that I can hear his calculated breathing. A set of white earbuds dangle down from his ears across his chest, ending somewhere below the belt line. I lose concentration around his midsection, completely distracted by the droplets of sweat taking a ride down the cuts of his stomach. May mercy be on my soul for the thoughts that start running through my head to the soundtrack of Marvin Gaye.

It's getting to the point where I'm most likely standing with my tongue curled somewhere by my feet, so I shake my head and rip my eyes up to his, which—not surprisingly—

are already looking at mine. I feel the cheesiest smile form on my lips and I squeak out an overly-cheerful, "Good morning!" My first words to him and they come out like a dreamy-eyed, teenage version of myself. I plan to smack my forehead when I head back inside.

The only acknowledgment I get from him is a tilt of his lips as he passes, showing me parts of his white teeth and creasing his cheek with smile lines that indicate he is most likely in his married years with kids in school and a dog in the backyard—something else I've often wondered. There's no ring on his hand, but he gives off the vibe that he'd be a killer soccer dad. Good on him for maintaining the twenty-year-old body. I lost that at twenty-two when my love for donuts became an obsessive affair.

I let out a little laugh at myself for being so Anastasia Steele, hoping that in my three seconds of eye sex that I didn't bite my lip, and I shake my head and take another succulent sip of my birthday treat, debating on if I should say something else to him before he jogs out of sight. There is always tomorrow, I suppose.

He stops mid-jog at the end of my property line. I watch his back rise and fall with his labored breathing, enjoy another drop of sweat as it rolls down the line of his spine, and then suddenly he's turning and running back toward me.

My eyes widen and my heart jumps from quiet and steady to loud and terrified, and my feet glue to the grass underneath them. In less than a second he's gone from attractive possible fling to scary man who can outrun me.

My fingers curl around my mug, knuckles turning white.

He stops in front of me, eyes locked on mine. The blues of his irises are so dark in color that I think they'll be haunting my REM cycle tonight—if I make it to a REM cycle.

He plucks the earbud from his right ear, grinning at me again, but he's so not putting off the father-of-the-year vibe anymore, so I'm unsure of what to think. I can't think *at all* with my heart pounding so loudly.

"Good morning," he says, his voice lighter and more cheerful than I expected, and it relaxes my heart and butterflies start to come alive in my stomach. He reaches up and I flinch, and the moment I do he pulls away.

"Sorry… you just have…" He nods to my nose, and I blink, hurriedly swiping at it. A deep, baritone chuckle falls off his lips, and he says, "Almost got it. You mind?"

He raises his hand again, and it takes me a couple of beats before I nod, excitement ripping up through my chest at the fact that he'll be touching me. The pad of his thumb runs over my nose, and he pulls it back with quite a hefty dollop of whipped cream that I have no idea how I could miss.

I let out a shaky laugh. "That's not embarrassing."

He smirks as he wipes it off on the waistband of his steel jogging shorts. "I'd call it cute."

Okay, not married. I'm going to believe he's not married and he's flirting with me. I should tell him not to charge a woman before attempting a flirtatious endeavor. But before I can get a word in edgewise, both his hands find my cheeks and then he's… *kissing* me.

There's no response time. No time for a slap or a moment of weakness to actually consider kissing him back. No time at all it seems. One second I'm being kissed and the next he's pulling back, a look of shock settling in his eyes before he shakes his head, drops my cheeks, and runs off my lawn and down the street. I watch his blond head bob out of view, my arms stuck out to my side like a complete fool, coffee in one hand, mail in the other. My mouth is stuck in a puckered position, lips tingling like they may have had action but they aren't exactly sure yet. The very small morning breeze is blowing up my overlarge hoodie, cooling my lady nethers and making me slowly wake up from the bizarre exchange.

My feet finally start listening to my brain, and I fumble my way back inside. Tom looks up from his spot on the floor, the sun making his black fur look glossy. He blinks and I let out a confused laugh.

"Well, that's a new one."

2

Scream Queen

"Sorry!" my sister-in-law Katie says as she hurries through my door with a car seat over the crook of her elbow, a diaper bag slung over her other arm, and a two-year-old clutching her forefinger. I quickly take the car seat holding my newest nephew and let her drop her Mom Luggage onto my couch.

"Chase here decided to poop all over his new outfit with a million snaps the second I got him strapped in the car," Katie rushes out, taking off her jacket with a skill only a mom can have with a toddler still clinging onto her hand. "You'd think I would've learned from the first kid to only dress babies in onesies before going anywhere."

I nod like I know what she's talking about (I don't). I just want to hold the baby, so I crouch down and unbuckle the little pooper, grateful he's already gotten that out of the way.

"Okay…" Katie breathes out, clapping her now-free hands together before bending to her bag. "I brought chocolate and red velvet because you have a thing for both, and raspberry filling for whatever you decide on. What one are you cravin...*don't lick the cat, Claire!* I can do one or the other or both."

She grins as she holds the cake mixes up, and I give her a look that answers the question she should've already known the answer to. She laughs and takes both boxes to the kitchen while I finally get little Chase unhooked from his car seat and watch Claire spit out cat fur onto my freshly shampooed carpet.

"Naughty pants," I tease my niece with the nickname I gave her as soon as she came out of utero and yanked seven hairs clean from my head. Katie had a homebirth—and I will not relive witnessing that experience— and as soon as little Claire was out, my brother Jim handed her to me—the woman with the towel. If you don't think it's possible to get beat up by a newborn, I have proof—in the form of a cheek scar— that it is *inarguably* possible.

I snuggle Chase in his deep blue fleece blanket, Eskimo kissing him as I follow the clang and crash sounds coming from the kitchen. Now this baby... he's the only one who's come close to convincing me that kids aren't so bad. The quiet cuddler, the fresh baby smell, and the perfect softness... sigh. It's tempting to try to make one of these guys for myself.

"Claire!" Katie scolds without even turning around from the cupboard. "Put the marker down."

I whip around to see my niece, Sharpie poised up against my wall. Her sweet face contorts into a red fit of rage as she chucks the open marker across the floor before falling

flat backward against the tile. The high-pitched scream is
enough to wake a dead man, but little Chase must be used to
it because all he does is stir a bit before snuggling back into
my chest. Katie continues pulling out ingredients as if
nothing is going on around us.

I'm instantly reminded why kids are not for me.

"You going out tonight?" Katie asks, eyes flicking up as
she sets a metal bowl on the counter and reaches for the cake
mixes.

I nuzzle my nephew, shaking my head and saying in a
baby voice I only pull out in front of present company.
"Auntie Maya wants to spend her birthday lounging around
her house, yes she does." Katie must not have heard the
grumble in my voice when she told me she was coming over
and that meant I had to put clothes on.

Katie lets out a long sigh, dumping the mix into the
bowl and dusting the counter top with red powder. "I would
pay for a birthday like that."

Claire's screams change pitch, and one more decibel
higher and only dogs will be able to hear her.

"I can't imagine why," I tease, then press a kiss to
Chase's head and swivel around to take a seat at my dining
table. The first few times Katie made my birthday cake for
me, I stood around asking if I could help with anything with
awkward, mumbled words. Now that it's an annual thing—
and we're much closer now—I pull up a high-backed, velvety
dining chair and chat while she experiments. She used to
make every cake from scratch, but since the kids came, box
mixes have become the norm. I'm *not* complaining; cake is

cake, and I'm thrilled to have a sister-in-law who cares enough to feed me chocolate even in her chaotic life.

"Want to hear a funny story?" I ask, settling in with Chase in my seat.

"Always."

"I got kissed this morning."

Her eyes widen, and she accidentally cracks egg shell into the bowl. "Oh! Did Vince come over?"

It takes everything in me to not respond with, "Who?" *Vince, Vince...* do I know a Vince?

Katie laughs, my confusion obviously written all over my face. She shakes her head and looks down at the cake mix as she picks out the shell pieces. "Well, that explains why I never heard anything about... *Claire! Please stooooop...* that particular date from *either* of you. I guess I have to take matchmaker off of my resume."

My niece finally eases up, flopping her arms down on the tile and silently huffing at the ceiling. If the girl had a white flag, it would soon rise above her defeated little body. With the sudden drop in noise, my brain is able to conjure up a blurry memory of a blind date I had not too long ago, but obviously long enough.

I laugh at myself, giving Katie an apologetic grin. "Right... Vince. He was... fun."

"You're a horrible liar."

"Only with you." She should see me in my realtor's blazer. I could sell a sandbox to a fish.

She rolls her eyes and searches for a whisk. "So, who was he?"

"He's... well, I'm not really su—"

A tug on my pant leg pulls my attention down to my niece and her watery eyes.

"Neeta darou wing. Pweese?"

I raise an eyebrow to the two-year-old translator. Katie leans against the counter as she stirs. "Do you have anything she can color on?"

"Drawer right by your hip. I should have some notepad paper in there." I've long since learned not to ask how in the world she knew what the toddler was saying. Moms have super powers—ones I cannot fathom ever possessing.

"Here you go, sweetie," Katie says, handing over a notepad and the attached pencil. I smile at the fact that she still calls that screaming child "sweetie." Katie tells her to go color at the coffee table in the other room, and then she turns to me. "Sorry. You were kissed this morning...?"

"Yes." I pause not only for emphasis, but to leave room for any more possible interruptions. "By a new neighbor I've spoken maybe four words to."

She jerks her head, her nose wrinkling upward as if the cake was suddenly made with rotten eggs. "Please elaborate."

I lean in, granting her request, even telling her in great detail the cut lines on this man. She listens with intense fascination, stirring the cake batter so lazily that I bet the ingredients could easily be separated. I'm not much of a story teller, never having stories to tell, so I really get into this one. After all, it's not every day you get kissed by a Grecian God.

"Wow," she says, her voice still laced with shock. She pushes up off her arm, straightening to mix the batter accurately now that I'm done talking. "I hope he doesn't have herpes."

I snort, but there's a plunge in my stomach that makes me shift Chase in my arms. That would be just my luck; I better keep my lips away from the baby until I know I'm in the clear.

"What'd you say to him?" she asks as she digs for a cake pan in the drawer under my oven.

"Nothing. He took off before I even realized what was happening."

She sets the glass pan on the counter and nibbles on her bottom lip. "Hmm."

"What?"

"Maybe we should stay with you tonight."

Claire starts singing with her very powerful vocal chords from the other room.

"I'm good. I really think he's harmless."

"I'm worried."

I smile. "You're *always* worried." I nod to Chase in my arms. "I think it's in your job description."

She gives me a look like she wants to argue, but she isn't going to. Thankfully the conversation is interrupted again… this time by me.

"Oh, it's Sarah," I say, looking down at my buzzing phone. "Give me a sec."

Shifting Chase, I push up off the chair and take the call in my living room. It must be big news if Sarah's calling on my day off *and* my birthday. I anxiously swipe the answer button.

"Hey!"

"It's a big one, Maya," she says, getting right down to business; it's why we get along. "The buyer's coming in early tomorrow, looking for someone to help him buy a property up on Rose Summit."

My heart soars up into my throat. "What time?"

"He scheduled an appointment at 7:30, but I'd get here at—"

"7:00. Yeah, I'm on it. *Thank you.*"

"No problem, boss."

I click off and happy dance with my phone in one hand, newborn nephew in the other. Rose Summit is full of million dollar properties. Multi-million dollar properties. The commission on that sucker... hello vacation!

The beeps from my oven timer sound through the room, and a few seconds later Katie appears in the archway, wiping her hands off on her jeans. "We've got a little bit. Did you record The Bachelor?"

"*MOM!*" Claire screams from the formal living room. "Leru a poopa fleur."

Katie sighs, her shoulders slumping as she's summoned. She points to the remote, silently telling me to at least get the show started, before she trudges her way to her toddler. And though I still didn't catch what Claire was saying, by the look on my sister-in-law's face, I'm pretty sure I really don't want to know.

3

Fumble and Mumble

"Chai Tea with cinnamon, cappuccino with chocolate shavings, and dark mocha with hazelnut." Sarah rotates the cups in the holder as she announces my choices, greeting me right off the elevator. Much to my delight, she's thought of every one of my personalities this morning.

I push open the glass door that leads into our offices, holding it open for her. Her thick heels clack against the floor as she scurries through, and I pluck the cappuccino from the container before she ends up spilling the drinks to the floor; she had me at chocolate shavings, and I don't want to see them all over the linoleum.

"His name is Cooper Sterling," Sarah rattles off. "According to the articles I found on him, he and his brother partnered in advertising and made their first million fresh out of college. Cooper acts as CFO, and invested the money *very* wisely."

I chuckle around my cappuccino. "Apparently. Did you get anything on his family life?"

Sarah dodges around a small trash can the cleaning crew must've left out. "He's thirty-two, single, and as far as I know, currently unattached at the moment. He likes to buy and flip properties on the side… He's got a home in LA and one in Texas."

"And he's looking for a realtor?"

"I assume it's a licensing issue. There's no record of any properties here, which is probably why he needs someone local."

A sly grin pushes at the corners of my mouth. "This is gold," I tell her. I've hit the jackpot of all clientele—rich, business savvy, and it doesn't hurt that he's in my age and relationship status bracket. It's a rarity for me to speak to someone who doesn't have a love interest or a few spawn running around at their feet.

"Is he here yet?" I ask.

Sarah shakes her head, her long, red hair waving over her shoulders. "No one knows about the appointment." Her lips turn up into a shy, almost shameful grin. "I just happened to be the person who delivered Parks' itinerary yesterday."

Garrison Parks, CEO of the now billion dollar corporation I work for, likes to meet the high-profile clients in person before he sets them up with one of the realtors. It is not my fault if I manage to bump into those clients before the meeting and put on a little charm.

I pick up my pace, Sarah's short legs jogging to keep up. "Will you call Mr. and Mrs. Bloomsbury and tell them you'll be starting the open house this morning?"

There's a hiccup in her step. "Um, Maya... I haven't run an open house solo yet."

"You've got this." I hip check my office door open with a grin. "Oh, and leave the Chai will you?" I've got plans for it that may or may not involve ruining my Ann Taylor blouse. The commission will make up for it.

Sarah sets the tea down on my very unruly desk, next to a stack of business cards that just came in on Friday. I pluck one up and tuck it into my jacket pocket. I don't usually need the card, but it's always good to have a backup in case I'm not memorable enough. The last time I snagged a highly-sought-after buyer, the couple didn't even make it to Parks' office before hiring me. What can I say... when you give up on marriage and family— the life I'd always assumed I'd have at thirty—you get really good at your job because it's pretty much all you have.

Sarah tosses the cup holder into the garbage, taking the hazelnut coffee and putting it to her lips. She reassured me months ago that she always orders something she wouldn't mind drinking. Her first week I agonized over being one of *those* bosses. Thankfully that guilt is nonexistent for the time being.

I take one more pull from the cappuccino before swapping it for the tea, adjusting my blazer and popping the top from the cup just enough that if someone were to... say... run into me... Whoops! There goes my drink.

Hey, it may be an oldie, but it's proved effective.

Sarah gives me an encouraging sort of look, showing me all the whites of her teeth. "Good luck."

She doesn't say it out loud, but she knows that I really need this one. It's been an extremely slow month, and there is a certain vacation I plan on taking when I can afford it—after all, a girl only gets one Dirty Thirty, and I don't mean the mess my niece left on my coffee table last night.

Mr. Parks' office is two floors above mine, and since there is no logical reason for me to be up there, I have to either make one up, or force the buyer onto my floor. Oh, there is a science to this ploy, and I've been conducting experiments and concocting hypotheses from the moment I witnessed Atticus Lovell swivel his way into a quarter-million-dollar-based commission seven years ago. He was a real estate god, retired at fifty-three, with homes in Paris and New York. He wines and dines nightly, never tied down—Atticus' only love was his 105 pound pit mix—and living out exactly what I'd like in life. I imagine some chic version of a cat lady in my case, however.

I take the stairs down to the lobby, peeking at the empty front desk. Our receptionists don't come in until quarter to nine—when they're on time—so I casually stroll to the floor indicator right next to the elevators. It's surprising they don't have these locked up after all the times I've pulled this move. I must be stealthier than I thought.

The metal screeches as I slide the name plate of my CEO and switch it with the realty offices. After a quick text, Sarah will head down and put them back in their correct placeholders before the offices are officially open. None will be the wiser.

I take a step back, a satisfied sigh floating from my

smiling mouth. Images of what I could do with a commission like this flick through my head like a movie montage—sunbathing in Tahiti, drinks in Cabo, perhaps. Places warm and free of noise and family pushing me into relationships. Oh, I'm not saying I'll be alone in paradise. No… finding a tanned Adonis would be ideal, someone who I flirt and play with for a week before heading back to my house for a stay-cation. I'll tell my family I'm still out, and I could park my booty on the couch, make every day a Naked Sunday, and watch guilty pleasures with Tom and Kat.

The elevator dings, and I shake out of my Tahitian fantasy. I hold the door open with my Coach heels and swap the name plates in there before sending it to the top and doing the same thing with the twin elevator. My phone buzzes, letting me know it's 7:20, and I need to get back upstairs.

I take the stairs, careful with the accident-ready tea, and position myself to be casually walking by the elevator when the doors open. That's step one.

Step two: The bump. Get Chai all over Ann Taylor.

Step three: The apology. Laugh it off, and if he's gracious, he'll be polite about it. If he's not, apologize to *him*.

Step four: The lending hand. Pretend confusion when he says he's looking for Parks' office. When he indicates he's on the right floor, enter the elevator with him.

Step five: The shut in. Keep up conversation until the doors have closed you inside with buyer.

Then it's all up to the gods. If I've been charismatic

enough, I seal the deal. All I'm doing now is being *memorable* without seeming pushy. It may be a little unorthodox, but it works, and I'm not technically breaking any realtor code.

I blow out a breath and watch the clock on one of the front desks tick the minutes away. My heart beats a little harder the closer it gets to the appointment time. Being a punctual person, when people aren't at least five minutes early, it gives me the annoyance itches. It's come to the point that I need to tell my siblings an inaccurate event time due to the fact that they do not share this particular peeve. A few years back I got into quite the quarrel with my sister Julie over this topic. She was ten minutes late for a dinner party *she'd* set up so I could meet whatever guy it was that time around. The fella and I had no chemistry, and I was left to my own awkward devices while we both waited for her and her husband Nathan to arrive. During the traditional bathroom trip after the main course, I lost it, letting her know that I was tired of being disrespected every time she showed up late. She then broke down and said I didn't know what it was like, waiting for the sitter, going over emergency protocol, worrying every second if being out meant being a bad mother. I chalk that argument as the moment of striking realization that my sister and I led very different lives. It was a blow at the time. I'm happy to say I'm content in the life I've chosen now. Not as resentful.

My newly manicured nails drum lightly against the to-go cup in my hands, my foot tapping in an impatient rhythm as the clock ticks from 7:30 to 7:31. If the buyer wasn't a brilliant paycheck, I'd probably ditch out. Yes, I really am that neurotic about punctuality.

The elevator dings, and my heart stops its unusual pattern. Before I took an interest in real estate, I'd been fond of the stage, so my acting isn't completely amateur. I learned that it's a key ingredient in my salesmanship.

The doors open, and I wait until I see a grass-stained Reebok step onto the floor. Interesting choice—I expected shiny and polished footwear. Maybe this isn't the buyer… and I curse myself for realizing the flaw in this particular plan; I'd completely spaced asking Sarah for a physical description.

I flick my gaze up to his face, hoping for a lost puppy look in his expression, only to come to a complete halt.

There is about a single day's old scruff on his chin, he's donning a baseball cap over his dark blond locks, and he's wearing a shirt. But other than those few details, he's a dead ringer for my drive-by kisser. His blue eyes slowly swivel around the floor, thick brows pulling inward. It's the lost puppy, but I've suddenly forgotten my entire five-step program.

In a moment of brain inactivity, I turn on my heel so quickly that I do exactly what I'd intended, just not in exactly the intended fashion—the tea splashes from my cup and onto the office linoleum, making my quiet exit very noisy.

A deep, friendly chuckle sounds from over my shoulder, sending a flock of appreciative wings through my midsection. I can't quite say if it's attraction because I've been fantasizing about him for about a month, or if it's because he's a man and that laughter sound just does something to a girl, but I feel I have to cover a blush that's rising up the back of my neck.

"Whoops," he says. A swish of jeans and the thud of his feet against the floor follow. I let out a very breathy laugh before turning to face the inevitable awkwardness that is about to ensue.

He's not looking. God has given me a pass because it gives me time to fix the expression on my face. I push away my shock and try to go about this as if nothing weird has happened between us at all. He's pulling tissues out of a box from Phil's desk, one right after the other quick as lightning. *Swish, swish, swish.*

His knees crack as he crouches down, and through my muddy thoughts I allow myself a grin. Creaky bones doesn't always come with age; it's usually coupled with a lack of stretching, as I discovered in my late twenties. Maybe he hasn't gone on his run today.

He's taken every tissue left from the box, so on top of feeling off my game, I'm now useless in cleaning up my own mess.

"Those lids are unreliable at best," he teases, tossing the soppy tissues into Phil's trash can. My ability to humor him has flown out the window, along with any professionalism I may have possessed.

"You... you're the..."

"Cooper," he finishes with a heart-melting smile. He sticks his hand out to shake only to realize it's gotten a bit moist from clean up duty. A low chuckle shakes his shoulders, and he wipes the tea residue onto the butt of his jeans. "By any chance do you know where Garrison Parks' office is? He said it was right off the floor, but… obviously…" He waves a hand around at the clutter of agent desks. His eyes indicate no familiarization, absolutely nothing to the fact that he's face to face with the woman he's been jogging past every day for the last month, not to mention, the woman he kissed on his morning run *yesterday*.

The skeptical part of me perks up, knocking at the corners of my brain. Maybe I'm seeing things. "Two floors up," is all I can mutter, pointing one finger sky high. My brows knit together, studying his features as thoroughly as I can before he's back on the elevator. Maybe it's a totally different man. A doppelganger at the least. Does insanity come standard at thirty? I was told it only creeps up on those with "Mom" brain.

He nods, taking a long step backward into the elevator and pressing the button on the side. I tilt my head, noticing how similar in body type, the hair, the smile lines—I won't ever forget those smile lines.

"Thanks," he says. The doors start to close, his face morphing from casual to apologetic in the last second. "And I'm really sorry about yesterday."

The relief I feel in the realization that I'm not losing my mind is short-lived, quickly replaced by irritation. His apology is the last thing I see in his blue eyes before he's on his merry way to the correct floor. *No, wait!* I have questions. Many, many of them.

My reflexes certainly aren't what they used to be—by the time I scurry over to the up button, the elevator has already ascended. I let my head fall against the metal doors and bang it a few times. What just happened was definitely not one of the steps.

4

Backfire Hire

Improvisation is my forte, and you bet your bottom dollar I play it to my advantage. But Cooper Sterling has thrown me a massive curve ball, one I can't seem to recover from even an hour after our encounter.

"It was a level beyond awkward," I tell Sarah, pacing behind my desk in my bare feet. "There's not a chance I'm getting that commission."

Sarah bites her lip, most likely masking her amusement at the disarray of my appearance. The hour has given me ample time to pull my curled hair from its up-do, leaving it frayed and haggard. I've talked my lipstick clean off, my once crisp business look is now hanging loose, my top buttons undone in an attempt to breathe. This is how I deal with embarrassment, confusion, and when things do not go according to plan—destroy the wardrobe!

"Well, you've got the open house," Sarah attempts an encouraging sort of smile. I'm sure she's pinning my reaction as an *over*reaction, but she doesn't have all the information.

Losing a big client happens every day—that's not what I'm concerned about at the moment.

I blow out a breath, setting my hands on my waist as I study the view from my teeny tiny office window. I used to have a direct line to the city park—trees, joggers, birds, a pond. It was all very cathartic until they built Almonte's, a Mexican eatery that, while very delicious, doesn't give off the same vibe.

I tilt my head and snatch my cell from my desk.

Any chance we can move the date to tonight? I can meet you at Almonte's after work.

It may not be the ideal place to woo a potential suitor, but it will ease my mind if I have plans tonight instead of dwelling on this insanity. I send the text off to Julie and then let the phone drop back on top of my messy desk.

"Should we do lunch?" Sarah asks, dragging her finger across her open iPad. "We have a bit of time between 1:00 and 3:00."

"I thought Thomas was taking you out."

She laughs me off. "I eat with my husband every day."

I let out a small chuckle at her enthusiasm to ditch her hubs. Sarah's in the honeymoon stage of her relationship as far as I can tell, even with the three kids—two with other men and the baby with Thomas. He slipped a ring on her finger late last year. He's currently out of work, which is why Sarah finds herself with me more than him—she's running herself ragged here—and I'm about to point that out when line one on my phone lights up.

"Maya?" Garrison's voice comes from the speaker. My

eyes turn to full moons, and I flick them up to Sarah donning an equally moon-struck expression.

"Um, yes Mr. Parks?"

"Are you available to run up to my office?"

Why? I feel like squeaking out at my boss. Instead I answer with a not-so-suave, "Sure thing," and then the line goes dark again.

"Maybe you were more memorable than you thought," Sarah says, excitement making her spine straighten in her seat. My stomach feels like it's about to drop straight out my ass.

I take a deep breath and start toward the elevators when Sarah clears her throat and nods to my lack of footwear. Right… even if the boss wants something as menial as paperwork—which I doubt—I should probably show up in shoes.

After slipping on my heels, I clack my way to the elevator, heart thumping in a cadence much faster than my gait. Perhaps Mr. Kissy Face has already left—meetings like his rarely take longer than an hour, and it's the only thing somewhat calming the jitters crawling under my skin.

The metal elevator doors shut me in, and a jolt runs through my stomach when I catch my reflection. I look as if I'm about to travel down the street in the infamous walk of shame. My fingers fumble around the hem of my shirt as I attempt to tuck it back into place, shakily trying to smooth out the fabric bumps in my pencil skirt. There is no hope for my hair. My stomach dips as the floor numbers tick upward, and I yank the pins from my frayed bun, bending at the waist and flipping my hair back and forth like a maniac, hoping that when I rise it gives off a wavy, relaxed effect. I only end up with a "just out of bed" version... which is a tick worse than where I was before.

"Grabubble," I growl, the intelligible expletive covered by the ding of the elevator hitting Parks' floor. I hurriedly fasten my hair at the nape with my elastic, unable to see the outcome as the reflective surface disappears into the walls.

"Maya," my boss says, an unusual smile set on his clean-shaven face. It's not as if Garrison and I don't get along; it's just normally, business is business, and I don't get a such a friendly greeting. My eyes drift from my boss's rare grin and stop on the man sitting in front of Garrison's massive desk. I step off the elevator, wobbling in my carelessly strapped on heels. Cooper rises from his seat, a dimple creasing in his cheek. I'm reminded of the first time I saw that sucker, and I clench my knees together.

"Mr. Sterling, this is Maya Baker." Garrison chuckles. "Is she who you're looking for?"

My eyes widen, my spine straightening. Paranoia will kill me some day. I curl my shaky fingers into balls, begging them to calm down long enough to shake Cooper's hand. His skin is rough, nothing I'd expect from a billionaire. Then again, his attire isn't what I'd expect either.

"Nice to formally meet you," he says with a knowing grin, one that makes my skin run a degree hotter, but my blood ice over. I still have no clue what to think of him, and if he thinks money and a rugged demeanor will drop my guard, he better think again.

"Maya," Garrison interrupts as Cooper drops my hand, "Mr. Sterling is looking for a property up on Rose Summit."

My eyes swivel to Cooper, who finds my expression laugh-worthy.

"It's a long story, but there is a place I've had my eye on, but it sold before I could get my shit together and hire a realtor. I found another one yesterday, so..." He spreads his arms out. "Here I am... hoping it hasn't been sold yet."

A wave of relief hits—this is business talk, which I can handle if I can get a grip on myself. I clear my throat and put on my realtor's smile. "Are you not looking to build?" With a bank account like his, I expected to sell him *property*, not a home.

The two men chuckle, apparently having already gone over this.

"I'm not exactly thrilled about that idea." Cooper scratches the back of his cap, exposing a toned tricep to match the rest of his upper body.

I take in a deep breath and shake myself into business mode. "I'll call the seller..." I say to Garrison, drifting off as I see him shaking his head.

"Before you jump the gun, Mr. Sterling has a few conditions before he hires you."

I raise an eyebrow, and Cooper laughs.

"He makes them sound frightening." Cooper reaches for his jacket hanging over the back of his seat. "I was just going to take you out first."

My paranoia rushes back, so much so that I trip backward into the elevator doors. "Um..."

35

"I mean to brunch or something," he clarifies with an embarrassed glint in his ocean eyes. "Talk about what I'm looking for. Maybe… *clear up* a few things."

Garrison levels me with a look, telling me silently not to blow this deal. I don't need the encouragement, however. A chance to clear things up sounds golden to me.

I straighten, smoothing my impromptu ponytail over my shoulder. "No."

Cooper's eyes widen, a bushy eyebrow arched at my bluntness. I allow myself a small laugh at his expense—it's nice to know I can throw him off his guard.

"I'm taking *you* out."

5

Wine and Dine

There's a place a few blocks south of the office, walking distance, really, which was nice because we took a car service and there wasn't time for any conversation. Plus, having a witness in the front seat was appreciated. I excel at small talk, part of my training. Cooper, however, acted as if he'd never used a car service in his life. Doubtful—he probably is escorted everywhere he goes. Maybe I make *him* nervous. The thought is oddly satisfying.

He looks up from his menu, placing it thoughtfully against the table. He hasn't said much so far, and it doesn't take me long to switch roles with him. I set my glass down with a suddenly shaky hand.

"I'm a family man," he says, throwing me in a spinning loop-dee-loop.

"Okay…" I say, grasping at whatever direction he's going. "So you want rooms for kids?"

He smirks, the scruff on his chin catching my attention and sending an unexpected jolt near my bellybutton. "I do, but that's not why I bring this up."

He settles his elbows on the table, reaching up to scratch his ear, and I tilt my head; I wonder if that's a nervous tick of his. "I have a blurting problem."

"Apparently."

"And I say a lot of things I shouldn't. I do a lot of things without thinking and then I over-analyze later. I've been jogging down your street for twenty-two days, and I'm not normally so flustered around a woman, but..." He waves his hand at me like I should know the end of his sentence.

I give him a look like I've eaten something sour and prod, "But...?"

He grins. "You are *insanely* attractive."

My nose rumbles, a snort billowing out just to emphasize how "insanely attractive" I am. I think about my order—a bowl of fruit and a glass of water—something light because I'm packing pounds that are usually frowned upon in today's society. My hair is still left a mess from earlier, there's a tea stain I hadn't noticed until we were on the way here, and yesterday there was whipped cream painting my nose.

I push from my seat. If he thinks I'm going to sit through this bullshit, he's got another thing coming.

"Wait... I'm scaring you, aren't I?" he asks, his brows etched inward, giving off that "family man" vibe I'd first thought of when I saw him.

I pause, halfway between sitting back down and standing up. "Yes, to be frank."

"I'm sorry. I'm not good at... this part."

I ease my way back into my seat. "What part?"

"Talking." He laughs at himself, toying with the corner of his menu. "I'm a very forward person."

"You don't say," I joke, referring to not only his "blurting problem" but the kiss. The dimple in his left cheek dips in, and my stomach flutters start to relax. He seems to have found the casual air between us as well, leaning back in his seat.

"What do you want in life?"

"What?"

He grins. "I want a family."

"So you said."

"A wife, kids. I want people to love and to spoil. I want to go on long road trips where everyone fights, yet we still have a good time. I want three dogs and a big backyard. I see people with those things, and I can't help but think... yeah, I'm happy. But that? That's *joy.*"

I raise an amused eyebrow. "That's quite the Hallmark movie you described."

He laughs. "Maybe." He reaches for his hat, pulling it from his messy, blond head. His hand runs through the strands, temporarily distracting me from our conversation.

"So... I come off a little strong," he continues. "I'm not good at beginnings. Asking a woman out, dating, flirting... However, I think I'd be a great ender."

My eyes narrow as I process. His tactic feels like conversational whiplash. Have to say, never met one like him... and it's... well, it's adorable. "This isn't a business brunch, is it?"

An unexpected, yet *very* attractive blush rushes over his face. "It's all tied together, I promise. I thought I'd clear things up first."

"Honestly, I'm more confused than enlightened at this point."

He sits up. "All right... here it is. I was running yesterday, enjoying the scenery and trying not to get consumed with thoughts of whether or not the gorgeous woman who lives on my new route would be outside. I seriously considered avoiding her street altogether until I caught sight of her, checking mail on a Sunday, dancing with her mug and her nose painted with whipped cream. She finally said good morning as I ran past, and I nearly fell on my ass. I'd never heard a voice so beautiful, so enchanting, that I just... well... I kissed her, partly out of fear that I was imagining things, mostly because I'd lost my damn mind." He tilts his head as if he just spouted off something as trivial as the weather. "Now that I know she's very real, I want her to know where I stand in case I don't get another chance."

It takes me several moments to catch my breath, to process the words that are continuing to spin me around on a turn-table. I think I've found my exact opposite—a man with no pretense, no small talk or flirtatious dance. A man who just lays his entire hand on the table and hopes for the best. I admire that, even if I could never pull it off.

My breath comes out in a shaky *whoosh* as I reach for my drink. "'Forward' doesn't do you justice, does it?"

He grins, his tight shoulders relaxing in a stance that makes me wonder how many people are put off by his social faux pas. "I've been told."

The waitress chooses that very convenient moment to take our orders—I change mine to something much heartier than I'd originally planned. If he can be himself, then I damn well will be myself.

"Am I still scaring you?" he asks, concern swimming in his pretty blue eyes. If I found him attractive before, it is nothing to how I see him now.

"No." I let out a bemused chuckle. I used to dream of these impossible men. Men I'd convinced myself didn't exist. I did such a good job selling the concept to myself that I hardly believe a word coming out of his mouth, and even if I did believe him, I'm set in my ways.

I swirl my straw around in my glass of apple juice. "Interesting that you pick a woman who isn't interested in family at all."

The corner of his mouth twitches. "You a cat person?" he jokes.

"Yes, among other things."

"Cynic?"

"Maybe."

He leans forward, sending a rush of warmth through my abdomen. "Does it scare you? The thought of family, something steady?"

I take a sip from my juice to stall. Yes, the whole thing scares me. I've seen firsthand what that life looks like, how frazzled my siblings are with their little ones, how every day is scheduled around everyone else instead of yourself. I think of how I used to picture what Cooper described mere

41

minutes ago—a Hallmark movie, and I wanted it. But as time ticked on and I had no prospects, I planted my feet firmly in reality. My career is my family. It sounds pathetic said out loud, but it's where I found my happy ending.

I set my glass back down. "No," I lie, then let out a breath. "You're not much for small talk, are you?"

He shakes his head at the table cloth. "Told you, I'm a real amateur at beginnings."

"You going to propose by the end of this meal?" I tease. "Tell me you love me?"

He grins, settling back in his seat and stretching his arms behind his head. "You're making fun of me."

"Yes."

"That's okay. I know I'm unconventional."

"Are we going to actually discuss business now?" I push a smile back, oblivious to the natural way it forms even during this "unconventional" conversation.

He lets his arms drop. "I'm looking at the property up on Rose Summit, like Parks said earlier," he says, surprising me by diving in without argument. A wave of disappointment rushes over me, but I shake it off and straighten in my seat.

"I can set up a walkthrough," I tell him, bringing my phone to the table.

"I'm not married to it, though," he says as I drag my fingers around my keypad. "I wouldn't mind another property near that area if it becomes available."

I bite my lip in thought, pausing in my text message to the seller. That house is beautiful, and I don't mind showing

42

it, but there are several plots farther east that would give him privacy. Something quiet and spacious.

"How firm are you on not building?"

"Oh, I'm not budging on that."

"Why?" I go bold, since he's already started us off on that foot. His mouth turns upward into a slow, amused smile, and I figure he likes my approach.

"I'm not patient enough for that."

I let out a small laugh, going back to drafting my text. "With your bottomless pockets, it may be *faster* to build than to buy."

"I'm not creative enough either," he adds. "I didn't major in interior design, exactly. I know next to nothing about architecture, and I'm not great at making decisions based on concepts alone." His grin slips from casual to playful. "When I see something I like, then I go for it."

I gulp away a rush of arousal that went straight between my legs. What in the world?

"You... you can hire people to do all that for you," I tell him, clicking send on the message and setting my phone back on the table. When my gaze lifts to meet his, he's donning an amused and... enchanted expression. It's one I'm unsure if I should be flattered by or intimidated by. I'm leaning toward the former.

He shrugs, breaking eye contact. "Want to know how I reached financial stability?"

"I'm always in the mood for budgeting tips."

He smiles at my response, then waves me in as if he's spouting off monetary gold and I'm the only one privy to the info. "I only invest in things I know I want."

Our eyes connect, and I watch those dark blue irises twinkle in a way I've only witnessed from a few men from my past. The familiar caffeine bubbles of attraction rise up under my skin, drying my throat and wetting my appetite. I allow myself a moment to entertain naked ideas, most of which take place right here on this table.

I blink, shaking my head and pulling away. "And you don't want an interior designer? A gardener?" An off-sounding laugh escapes me. "I assumed you already had staff in spades."

"I believe in trying things yourself first." He takes a long pull from his water. "Only reason I hired a realtor is because I read about a page into a very thick book on buying a house before realizing it was not going to be something I could fudge my way through."

"Wise decision." I lean back as our waitress puts our food in front of us. A dip of guilt hits my stomach at the small error in judgment I had when I switched my order. Cooper, however, seems very excited about what I've chosen to eat, his blue eyes lit up as they scan over my hearty meal for more-than-one. He thanks our waitress and immediately reaches for one of my slices of bacon.

I tap his knuckles. "You have your own."

"Yours looks crispier."

I point a warning with my fork, and he laughs and settles in with his meal. The exchange has a strange aftertaste—strange because it doesn't *feel* strange. In my scarce dating life, I've yet to fight over food; it's not exactly something that happens early on. Another perk of only dipping your toes into relationships.

Yet, I don't seem to mind that it was his automatic response. Feeling brave and perhaps a little curious, I reach across the table for a succulent-looking strawberry sitting atop his three-stack pancake plate. He doesn't blink an eye as I fork the fruit and bring it to my mouth.

"You can answer that if it's important," he says, nodding to my phone. I blink away my fascination at his indifference to a near stranger picking from his plate and turn to my buzzing cell. It's Sarah, messaging every few seconds because the open house starts in twenty. I quickly message her to take point on it, then swipe over to the response to the house showing request.

"You're in luck," I tell him with a smile. "I can show you the house on Rose Summit this afternoon."

He grins over a mouthful of pancake, something I'd never in my life thought I'd find attractive, but he somehow pulls it off. "Wonderful."

I don't know how he did it, but now that the business portion is over—for the most part—I find myself hoping he brings up some more deep conversation. Not that one person has changed my stance on the subject; I'm more curious than anything else. I've never had these conversations, never gotten past the beginning to see what the middle or end even looked like. Ends to me played out like a mutual falling away once we realized we'd done all we could do with each other. I never felt like I was used and thrown away, because I never got close enough to someone to feel that way. I never wanted to. So why am I even considering talking about life, relationships, and the like with a man who obviously is heading down a different direction?

"Is there a policy against dating clients?" he asks, his mouth now free of food. I internally laugh at the relief I feel that he's back to being so blunt. It's mighty entertaining.

"It's frowned upon," I say, poking my fork into the yolk of my sunny-side-up. "But there's no official policy."

"Do you have your own policy against it?"

I slowly shake my head. "Haven't needed one."

"Hmm," he murmurs, returning to his food. "Interesting."

I set my fork down. "For someone who rarely beats around the bush, you sure know how to do so when it's the most annoying."

He laughs. "Well, I was waiting for the end of the meal to get down on one knee." He winks, and I shake my head at my plate.

"At least you're aware of your insanity."

The dimple on his cheek dips suddenly before fading out entirely. "To answer your previous question honestly, though... no, I won't be telling you I love you. *That* sentiment is something worth waiting for."

"Wow." I bite back a smile, hiding behind another sip of juice. "Something we agree on."

There's a nice, calming air between us that is somehow laced with a desire that I don't too often feel. He's pulled a one-eighty on my view of him with one simple meal. He's right about one thing—he's definitely a better ender.

46

6

Lip Tryst

"You look happy," Julie says, fixing her lifeless bangs on the other end of the screen. I prop my iPad up on its stand to free my hands up to flip through my wardrobe.

"It's a *huge* commission, Jules. I'm talking six figures."

Her eyes widen appreciatively. "Does that mean you're treating tonight?"

A euphoric laugh floats from my freshly glossed lips. "If you want." I will pay for her next grocery bill. Her next *seven* grocery bills, I'm that excited about landing this buyer. My high has nothing to do with how the attractive man thinks *I'm* attractive, too.

Nope, can't be that.

"I was kidding." She tilts her head back and forth. "Kind of."

I skate my fingers across a few blouses, pausing on a lavender one with a low dip in the front I haven't had the courage to wear, but after a morning of ego stroking, my confidence levels have spiked. I pull it from the hanger.

"Hang on a sec…" Julie says, and then calls off screen. "Did you walk the dog?"

My ten-year-old nephew Lucas answers with a grumble.

"No Wi-Fi password until it's done."

"Where's the leash?"

"Where'd you put it?"

"I don't know."

"Then I don't know." Her eyes follow across the room, and I know exactly what look her son is giving her by the way her lips purse. "Take Lauren with you!"

"Uggggnnn."

Julie turns back to me. "Sorry."

"No worries." Honestly, I'm used to it by now. Being the only sibling without kids has trained me enough to expect weird and frequent interruptions.

"Oh! Nate and I may have to duck out early tonight," she says. "The sitter can only stay till 9:30, and the kids have school tomorrow." She lets out a long, tired sigh. "I can't wait till summer's here. May is my least favorite month."

I drop the blouse onto the bed with a laugh. She says this every year, and two minutes into summer vacation, she's wishing them all back in school.

"That's fine." I grin and turn to my closet. "Maybe we'll want you out of there."

Her brows pull inward. "Is that genuine enthusiasm I'm hearing?"

I lift a shoulder. "Maybe." My hand smooths down one of my gray jackets as I consider pairing it with the lavender for the showing. "It's been a good day."

Her suspicious lips turn upward, seemingly excited about not only my compliance to go on this blind date, but my eagerness. I'm surprised by it, too, if I'm being honest. But Cooper's flattery has made me feel like a walking vixen, even if I'm not the girl he's looking for—which I did tell him.

"Good. I really think you're going to like him. He's funny, laid back, likes cats. Oh! And I've heard through the vine that he's… got no reason to compensate for anything if you catch my drift."

I tilt my head at her. "I know what overselling sounds like."

"Fine. I'll just leave you to confirm that particular rumor." Her laugh is cut off by an *oof!* as her three-year-old hops into her lap, and I get a shot of bushy brown hair through the screen.

"Eye-ah!"

"Hi Lily."

"Eye-ah, Eye-ah, Eye-ah," she sings, and the next thing I see is a thumb before the screen goes black. Squeals from my niece and scolding from my sister blend together as Julie chases her daughter around. I laugh and lean over my desk chair to reach the iPad.

"I'll see you tonight, Jules!"

"Bye!"

I click off the chat and swipe over to my schedule. Forty-five minutes till the showing, and a swoop of excitement rushes through my stomach. Cooper ended the brunch with a proposal—a business one. I'm officially his realtor, and as such, I think I'm still going to try to convince him to build. Partially for selfish reasons—when I can, I try to give Warren business. My best friend Holland married the contractor when I was still living in my crazy early twenties, and they're coming up on ten years of marriage and first born baby. She doesn't mention it much, but I can tell they're struggling a bit.

I tap in a reminder to give her a call, Kat hopping onto my desk and rubbing her head on my hand until I give in and scratch her ears. "Okay, troublemaker," I tell her, pointing to the bed, "stay off my clothes while I shower. Orange cat fur is not in this season."

She turns to show me her butt so I can give it a good scratching as well. Instead of granting her request, I strip down and head into my adjoining bathroom. My eyes narrow as I watch the kitten tilt her head at my bed where I've laid out my outfit. With a sigh, I grab my clothes and take them into the bathroom with me. My kitties are cute, but I don't trust them for a second.

***

The best thing about showing high-priced housing is that the owners keep it sparkly clean. There are a few showings I've done that we didn't even walk inside due to either the smell or questionable carpet stains.

I punch in the code and retrieve the key from the lock box. I'm a little early, so I let myself in and turn the security off with the number the seller's realtor gave me. The entryway has a simple elegance to it—a wide open space with a high ceiling and extravagant lighting. A grin teases at the corner of my lips. With Cooper's lack of filter, I imagine a very candid assessment of the place is coming, and since the owner's pretty darn well off, I bet there is a camera or fifteen capturing the walkthrough.

Allowing myself a little laughter over the thought, I clack my way into the formal sitting room and set my keys and purse on top of a polished white side table. The window runs from ceiling to floor, providing the room with a view of the city below. I don't blame him for wanting to look at the place—it has a je ne sais quoi outside of the lavish layout and fine furniture that gives a person a sense of calm and serenity. If I was a billionaire, I'd want something like this—but unlike Cooper's stubborn hide, I'd build one specifically made for me.

Speaking of stubborn billionaires, a mud-ridden truck pulls through the front gate, squeaking to a stop behind my—by comparison—teeny tiny VW bug. I squint, trying to decide what color the truck is under all the muck; I'm guessing deep purple? Deep enough to almost pass as black if it weren't for the sun streaking down against the hood.

Cooper shuts the loud engine off, cranking the door open and hopping from the truck's height. An involuntary gulp threatens in my throat, and I press a hand over my chest to calm the sudden skips in my heartbeat. It's ridiculous— these juvenile reactions to a man I know is *not* for me, but his candidness earlier has awakened a playfulness that finds little harm in playing the game, even if there is no winner at the end of it.

I take a deep breath to calm the flutters and put on a

winning smile. Cooper gets to the front door before I do, poking his head in and meeting my smile with one that would blow the panties off any innocent bystander.

"Afternoon."

"On time," I reply for lack of something clever to say. "I like that in a client."

He steps inside and flips his keys around his forefinger until he gets them settled into the front pocket of his jeans. "I've shown enough of my own houses to know what a pain it is to have to leave for showings."

"Thoughtful."

"Just another one of my finer qualities for you to consider," he says, leaning into me as he passes. I purse my lips to refuse him the satisfaction of amusing me with his arrogance. But it doesn't quiet the unsteady rhythm that's returned to my heart the moment his warm breath rushes over my shoulder. Damn him.

"Well, look at that view," he says, and I shake myself out of the daze I'm falling into and chant the dollar amount I'm hoping to get from this whole thing. *Professionalism, Maya. Learn to use it.*

Cooper crosses his arms over his white t-shirt, the muscles near his elbows are veined indicators that he either works a lot with his hands or he has a personal trainer—or is one. I fix the flowy hem of my blouse so that it hides my midsection roll more effectively.

He stands in front of the window and admires my personal favorite perk of the place while I confidently step up beside him.

"It's reflective," I inform him, veering into my realtor mode, imagining sunny vacation spots as soon as I get my commission. "Feel free to forgo the drapes."

His shoulders jerk with a hint of laughter. "Or parade around in the nude."

Mother of all sweet images. I fold my arms to stop the onslaught of jitters that run through my stomach just at the visual of Cooper in the emperor's new clothes, standing like Mr. Clean in front of this giant window while some innocent passerby hasn't a clue to the show they're missing.

I clear my throat. "Can't do that with a bunch of kids running around."

"Exactly." He leans to the side, his face creeping close enough to mine that I can count the individual tiny hairs along his jaw. "Gotta get that in before they get here. Stripped Sundays."

I bite back a grin. He has a much cleverer name for his own personal naked time. I plan on stealing it next "Stripped Sunday."

"How many floors?" he asks, turning from the window and crossing toward the stairs. After a few tripped steps to catch up with him, I slip my heels off near the front door.

"There's a basement, main level, second level, and a master suite that is the entire third floor. There's an attic as well."

He lets out a long whistle, pulling himself up the stairs using the banister. He takes them two at a time, and my plump and short legs scurry to keep up with his daddy long ones.

53

He stops at the second floor for only a moment, grinning as I let out a long breath as I reach the top, and then he starts down the hall. "Where's this third level staircase?"

"Not sure." I push open one of the doors that leads to a bigger-than-my-kitchen bathroom. "Did you want to see these rooms first?"

He shakes his head, blue eyes lifting to the ceiling. "I wanna see top to bottom." His gaze takes a swift turn toward me. "Just my style."

I wait for his stare to drop, hitching my hand on my hip in faux annoyance at his entendre, even though I'm enjoying them more and more, never having had this sort of attention directed toward me. But I warn myself to err on the side of caution until I can get a thorough background check on him—not that I am toying with ideas of actually giving in and agreeing to a date with the man.

He surprises me once more by not letting his eyes travel south, and he turns, starting down the hall again. My hand falls from my waist, and I blink against the surprising disappointment crawling through me. He starts opening random doors, and I join him, internally shouting at myself. I open doors to so many lavishly decorated rooms that I lose count after six.

"You'll definitely have room to grow," I say with an amused grin after shutting the door to another bedroom.

He laughs, and the sound swoops through my chest, and I bite my lip, forcing myself not to get giddy over the fact that I made that laugh happen.

"Ah," he says, distracting me from the doorknob I was about to try. He steps through the door he just opened, and I secretly appreciate the fact he's not insisting I lead him up. The curved stairwell is narrower than a standard staircases, and wiggling my plushed-out rearend in his face doesn't sound appealing to me in the slightest. The very opposite, very tight, very manly view he's providing me, however…

"Well," he says, letting out a long sigh as he steps into the master suite. "That's disappointing."

I meet up with him, desperately trying to hide the fact that my breathing is close to a woman in labor. My eyes scan around the suite, brows pulling in. What could *possibly* be disappointing? The furniture, maybe? The white-only color choice isn't my personal preference, but he has his own furniture to replace all of that. The windows are reflective up here as well, going from ceiling to floor facing the back side of the house which is just the rocky mountain wall. It gives the place a more private feel, for sure.

He strides toward the bathroom, the deep, jetted tub taking up most of the space—as it should—leaving a marble shower in the corner, his and hers sinks, and a private area for the toilet. He doesn't comment with anything but a "hmm" before moving onto the closet.

"This is the quietest you've been since we've met," I joke as he clicks on the light and walks through the giant closet that could very well double as a nursery… if that's what he wants. I'd use it for what it's designed for; maybe spend nights with my shoes. I mean, there's a spot right there that I could prop a pillow up and curl under a blanket with my brand new Manolo Blahnik's.

Yes, this closet is going to make it on my bucket list.

"I'm analyzing myself," he says, stealing my attention away from the rack of Prada bags I'm currently coveting. "Trying to decide if I'm being reasonable or too picky."

"Have you reached a verdict?"

He flicks the light off and heads back into the main suite. I silently say goodbyes to the shoes while he takes a stance in front of the window similar to the one he used in the formal.

"This view," he comments. "I expected something a bit more... well..." We simultaneously tilt our heads, which causes us both to grin, and only me to blush.

He lets out a gravelly sigh. "Just more."

He has a point; the view here is equal to staring at the side of a building wall, though this is mountainous rock instead of brick. Compared to the view of the formal, yes... there is something left to be desired.

"Can I be honest?" I ask him.

"Please."

"When buying a house, there are two things to consider," I say, turning toward him. His blue eyes are so intent on listening that my brain stutters. "You will not find the perfect house, but you will find something close to it. It's just a matter of figuring out what imperfections you can live with."

His jaw clicks, and he thoughtfully nods at the window. "Wise words." He slides a hand into his back pocket. "Mind if I take some pictures?"

"Go for it."

He holds the phone out, camera facing me, his lips forming into a playful grin. I shove his arm down and shake my head.

"Of the *house.*" My heart adds an extra beat when my fingers get the dose of warmth from their short and sweet contact with his skin. I'm reminded of the sweet way he wiped the whipped cream from my nose, the way my breath disappeared for half a moment of perfection.

He doesn't take many shots of the house, even as we make our way through the second level and the main. He pauses in the kitchen, setting his phone on the island and peering inside one of the ovens.

"Seeing if your head fits in there?" I tease.

He comes out with an achingly sexy smile on his face. "Well, besides the bedroom, the kitchen is my favorite room in a home."

"Because?" I ask, noticing he used the word "home" not "house." It's a very *family* word; I usually only hear it from buyers who are couples. Rare in a billionaire bachelor.

"Food," he says as if it's an obvious thing. "Preparing food, cooking food, baking food, *eating* food." He spreads his arms wide. "This is where the magic happens."

I bite back a laugh. "And the bedroom?"

"Magic happens there, too." He drops his arms, settling one of his hands on the oven door before pushing it back into place.

"Can't help yourself, can you?" I say, shaking my head.

"You just set it up so nicely." His eyebrow twitches.

"The honest answer? Sleep. Sleep happens there. Rest, rejuvenation… the start of a new day and the end of an old one. All in the bedroom."

He takes a deliberate step toward me, and a rush flows through my skin, as if I've been dipped head first into warm oil and set out in the sun to dry.

"Trying to wax poetic?" I try to tease, yet my voice has taken on its own version of staccato.

He shakes his head, blond hair tousling with the movement. "I like the idea of new days," he says, stepping ever closer. I feel as if I should step back, keep the distance between us the same, but my feet have melted into the floor. "That there's hope to start over when things don't necessarily go your way. Like when you hope you find that woman who will make every day worth getting out of bed… or staying in it. Whatever the mood calls for."

He stops in front of me, his stare heating up my already warm cheeks. His eyes explore my face, examining from the top of my crown, over my cheek bones, and down my nose to my lips. I feel like I should be self-conscious about it somehow—in fact, I expect the dose of insecurity— but…I've never felt so desirable in my life. My thoughts start to escape me, and I have to strain to focus on our conversation. What *were* we talking about? Bedrooms? Kitchens? No… mornings. We're on how he's a morning person. Just another thing we're polar opposites in.

A grin forms on his lips, letting that dimple arrive just in time to melt me completely.

"And food," he says, his body now a whisper away. "I

like the idea of food in the morning."

There is a likely chance that I am bewitched, because only a person under a spell would kiss a man who equally scares her as he does intrigue her. My bare feet have to push up on their very tiptoes to reach, and even then, my palm smooths over the back of his head to coax him to meet me halfway. He covers my mouth, and my lips aren't slow or shy—they are ready for some real aggressive action which his lips are more than happy to oblige. "Bewitched" doesn't even cover the electrified current running through my frazzled heart; my thoughts aren't even here on earth at the moment.

I feel his palm at the small of my back, reeling me in to the hard plate of his chest. He tugs at my bottom lip over and over, the softness of his mouth combined with the rough scruff of his chin elicit uninhibited moans from deep down in my fluttering stomach. My fingers curl into his shirt, the touch of this man annihilating every rational thought I know I should have. He's soft, he's rough, he's hard and warm and he's satisfying a long stint of loneliness and at the same time never quenching my thirst. I claw at him, wishing I hadn't chosen a pencil skirt when picking my outfit.

The fingers on my back squeeze me tighter for just a moment before he pulls back. His lips leave mine so suddenly that neither of us breathe right away. I let out a tiny sigh, embarrassment starting to creep its way up my neck, but his lips find mine once more in a softer, gentler embrace. It's only for a second, but it takes my breath away just the same.

He does it again. And another time. It's almost as if he

keeps talking himself in and out of the decision. A relieved smile slips onto my lips. It's good to know I wasn't completely out of line. Then again, he'd kissed me before we'd said a handful of words to each other. It's been at least twenty minutes before I lost control.

I search for something, *anything* to say; I don't blame him now for just taking off the last time this happened. How do you put a voice to a moment like this? How can you follow it up?

"I have a date tonight," I blurt out, picking probably the worst possible words I could have.

His eyebrows lift. "What about tomorrow night?"

I take a deep breath, letting it out through my tingly lips. "Depends on how well this one goes."

He laughs, and his hand falls from my back as I step away for some much needed clarity. "Oh, I already know how it'll go."

"Oh really?" My fingers fumble down my skirt as I attempt to straighten out not only my clothing, but my hormones. "Care to tell me?"

His head tilts in a playful, yet sexy manner, and he reaches for his phone. "Wouldn't want to spoil it for you." He slides his thumb around the screen. "Six-thirty tomorrow night work for you?"

Not willing to give him the satisfaction of knocking me clean out of my shoes—if I were wearing any—I collect myself and say, "If I don't have plans with Todd already." I have no idea if that's the right name.

"That's a yes, then."

"It's a maybe."

He slides his phone into his back pocket, then closes the gap we've put between us. I find myself slowly falling back into dangerous territory. He waits there, playing chicken with me until I finally break.

"What?"

A smile cracks on his lips. "Just hedging my bets." He steps around me, heading out of the kitchen and down to the basement.

"What's that supposed to mean?" I call after him.

He turns with that dimple in his cheek. "That tonight, when you're with him, I guarantee... you'll be thinking of me."

7

Blind Date Fate

As much as I'd hate to give Cooper the satisfaction of victory, I think he's earned it. Steve—his name is Steve, but Todd was close—crunches into another bite of his taco, breaking me from yet another train of thought that brought me to this afternoon in the kitchen.

It wasn't even a related topic, either. I struck up a conversation about dental floss, something I refused to believe would bring me to thoughts of Cooper. But the dental floss reminded me of the mint leaves logo, which turned into reminders of watering my plants out front. My thoughts then ran off with Tom and how he ate the last of my tulips when I let him out the other day. The cat needs to go on a diet, and I tried to think of what ingredients were in his food. I laughed silently at the thought of him turning away from dietary meal plans, and that he'd much rather go for whatever I had in my fridge. Which brought me to the lasagna I meant to put in the oven. Then I saw Cooper sticking his head inside the one at the showing today. The oven door closing, his slow, steady strides toward me, that dimple teasing me just seconds before…

"Oh shoot," Jules says, her eyes on her phone. I wonder when my thoughts wandered off again; I don't remember her pulling it out. "Katie says Lucy's out of diapers. I forgot to pick some up this afternoon."

Nate, my brother in law, wipes his chin free from his meal and sets the napkin on top of the table. "She needs one now?"

"She's currently in one of Claire's, and it's drowning her." Julie turns to us, the corners of her mouth dipped down. "I'm sorry… we should probably run…"

"Please," Steve says. "Go take care of Lucy."

I nod, reassuring my sister and the concerned look in her eyes. I wonder if she knows this isn't going very well. Though, that's hardly Steve's fault.

"Okay…" She rises from her seat, Nate holding her chair for her. I tilt my head at the insignificant action, realizing just how significant it really is. Cooper did the same thing for me at our brunch.

Jules leans over to give me a hug, whispering in my ear. "Talk to you tonight."

I smile and nod against her cheek. Talk to her about what, I have no clue. I don't know how much of Cooper I should divulge, if anything. She'd only get excited, encourage me to date him exclusively, get serious, say yes to proposals, and have lots and lots of babies. As interested as I am in getting closer to Cooper for a fun fling, he's not interested in *only* that, and honestly I should find a way to back out of tomorrow night before things go farther with him than they already have. Easier to preach than to practice, I'm afraid, especially when I keep thinking about that knee-wobbling kiss.

They leave the busy restaurant, and I put a smile on my face and hope to heavens I at least look like I'm enjoying myself.

"I figured something like that would happen," Steve jokes, nodding at my sister and brother-in-law's retreating backs. "My sister always has a sitter excuse when she sets me up."

A little laugh floats from my lips. "You get set up a lot, too?"

He leans in, his thick brows twitching as if he's sharing some type of secret. "*Always.*"

"At least I know I'm not with a blind date novice." I pick up my glass of water, attempting a flirtatious tone and hoping it stays with me throughout the rest of the meal.

"So," he says, leaning back in his seat and settling in with his taco. "How do you like selling houses?"

I shrug, smile fading at the change in subject, knowing it will inevitably bring on thoughts of Cooper. "It's interesting, for sure. Never the same clients twice."

"What's the worst client you've had?"

I clasp my fingers together to rest my chin on, toying with my bottom lip as I think on it. The question feels like part of an interview, even though I've been asked it many times, and with each new prospective dating partner, I've had a different answer. It's never bothered me before; I enjoyed the light-hearted, puddle deep conversations that surround the first date. I know all the answers, I know how to move my lips and kink my eyebrow at just the right moments. Steve isn't even that bad to look at—he's got great hair, strong arms, and he's not bad company either. It's just… lacking for some unapparent reason, and I feel as if I should blame a Mr. Cooper Sterling for that.

"The one I had today," I say, bitterness lacing into my tone. Steve's bushy eyebrow tilts upward, his mouth too full to vocally ask me to continue. "He's a picky billionaire, and very… blunt in his opinions."

He swallows. "That's a bad thing?"

"Annoying, I suppose." I'm lying through my teeth.

"Well, I hope for your sake he finds the right house soon."

He said house—a bachelor thing to say. I give the response way too much thought for what it's worth. I wish I could feel comfortable enough to ask what I really want to know—what is he looking for? Cooper came out and said it, his directness at first, surprising, but in hindsight… refreshing. But as I'm not looking for anything serious, I feel I can't talk about serious things with Steve.

I internally sigh at the fact that Cooper was so right, and I've spent most of the hour thinking of him, and I'm most likely destined to do so the rest of the evening. I take another sip of water, put on a polite smile, and try to do my best with the small talk I'm not so sure I like anymore.

"So… What do you do?"

***

My heavy front door clicks shut behind me, and I consider the kiss that just took place on my porch as I swing the deadbolt into its nightly position. My lips don't feel as if any attention was given, which is probably an accurate description. I think Steve was trying to make things quick, and the peck was more out of obligation than desire.

I fling my purse up on the hook by my door and slip out of my heels. I don't blame him in the slightest; I was just as dull of company as he was, if not more-so.

Hooking my fingers into the sling-backs of my heels, I pad my way through to the kitchen to stash my doggie bag, only to be stopped short by a dark gray-covered bottom.

"Hello?" I say, and the refrigerator raider peeks from under her extended arm.

"Whoa…" Holland says, straightening her spine. "9:15. Someone had fun."

I roll my eyes at my best friend's sarcastic smile and open the snack cupboard. "Looking for these?"

She practically drools a stain onto her pink tank top, reaching for the chocolate frosting and graham crackers in my hand. I pull back and gesture to my plushy couch where all our emotional eating happens. She grabs the milk while I get a couple of cups.

"Is Warren helicopter spousing again?" I ask, flumping into the cushions. Holland plops down next to me, setting the milk on the coffee table.

"He cleansed the entire house. If it's not baby book approved, it doesn't cross the threshold."

I pull the graham cracker sleeve open and quickly hand

her one. "Even the cookie stash?"

She nods, crunching into the cracker. "All four of them. You'd think *he* was having this baby."

"Well, he did help make it."

She snatches the frosting from me. "If you're going to calmly make logical points then I can no longer call you my best friend."

I smirk and lean back into the cushions, indulging in the sweet treat after a dud of a night.

"I'm finally past the puking part," Holland says, filling up a spoon with a glob of frosting. "I want to *eat*. I've missed chocolate. Raspberry sauce. *Cake*."

"I have all three of those things." I grin. "My birthday was just yesterday."

She turns a pair of brown bulbous eyes in my direction, spoon hanging from her mouth. I laugh at her obviously apologetic expression and dip my own spoon in.

"It's *fine*. I had an excellent day all by myself." Well, and my cats. Not to mention the drive-by kissing I started the day off with.

"I'm horrible," she croaks. "I'm forgetting *everything*, but I wasn't going to forget that. I wasn't." She grabs at her highlighted hair that needs a retouch, but the doctor advised against it, so Warren put his foot down. "I will make it up to you."

"Just help me eat that cake."

She lifts her reddened eyes. "Tonight?"

I snort around my spoon and shove off the couch. I've spent enough time around pregnant women to know that they are serious about food, that watery eyes happen for no reason, and they make for great company (and birth control).

"You don't have to..." she mumbles from the couch, watching me fish the cake from the fridge.

"It's good timing, actually," I admit, slapping my left butt cheek. "I need to add more cushion to my cushion."

Holland gives me a weird look, graham cracker dusting her lips. "Care to elaborate?"

"It's been an eventful couple of days."

She swivels in her seat so she doesn't have to crane her neck. "Ooh, my present to you... we're going to only focus on your drama this time."

Since I rarely have drama to focus on, I take her up on the offer. "You know how you loved the fact that Warren wanted to marry you right away and you were going to spend all your fun twenties experiencing things together and then have babies at thirty and grow old and have a porch swing and what-have-you?"

Her lips turn down in the corner. "This is not the deal I just laid out for you."

I lick a stripe of raspberry sauce off my finger and roll my eyes. "I was saying that I think I've met your husband's emotional doppelganger."

She nods toward the large slice I'm dishing for myself. "And you want to fatten up so he finds you undesirable, is that it? Not quite ready to settle down and too chicken to tell him?"

"Couldn't hurt."

Her mouth splits open with light laughter. "What'd you

68

into the conference room. The clock overhead ticks the first second into a very long eight hours of fluttering anticipation.

***

I pace a hole through my bedroom floor, holding my phone to my ear and yelling a very long message to Holland.

"You have exactly two minutes to call me back or else it'll be too late!"

I click off and toss the cell onto the bed by the opened UPS box. "This is crazy," I tell Tom who is lazily lying in the late day sun beams on my floor. "He can't be serious."

I pull at the fleece pajama bottoms—that surprisingly fit with the drawstring—and the graphic t-shirt that says "Cozy King." So much for the public place, fancy restaurant guy I pegged him for. Like with every other conversation we've had, he skips the formality and goes right into putting me in lounge wear. I don't care how much it smells like him, or how much it reminds me of his soft lips and scruffy chin and how, yes, my stomach cannot find a settled position just from the thought that maybe these are *his* actual clothes.

My hands flop down to my sides. "No," I say to my sleeping cat. "I'm not doing it."

I barely get a hold of the hem to yank the shirt off my body when the doorbell rings. He's early. He's an early man. Why does that turn me on so much?

I untangle myself from the material and march down the stairs. I make sure it's loud enough so he knows exactly what mood I'm in before I even open the door.

After fumbling with the lock, I swing it open and give him the best glare I can muster while simultaneously swooning at his trimmed chin and his matching pajama set.

"Explain," I bite out.

His eyes scan down my body, his lips twitching upward at the hitched hand on my hip. When he gets back to my face, I give him a look that reiterates my previous request.

"It suits you." He slides his hands into the soft pockets at his side. "You'll have to give me a minute here."

"For what, exactly?"

"To catch my breath."

Though the words are genuine, if not a little romance movie-esk, the effect of they have on me is a tad unexpected. My skin feels on fire, burning from somewhere deep inside my chest and simmering up to the surface. I hide it with a playful, derisive snort.

"I take it we're staying in tonight?"

He shakes his head, reaching out for my hand. "Nope."

Electric shocks skyrocket through my midsection the moment he entwines his fingers with mine, making me fumble over my words. "Hold on. We're going *out* in these?"

His smile deepens at my free hand pulling at the fleece. "Do you have something against sleepwear?"

"No..." I draw out, planting my feet firmly in my doorway as he starts leading me to his truck. "I just don't make a habit of it outside of these walls."

"I promise that where we're going, you'll want to be comfortable."

"I can be comfortable in a dress."

He grins and drops my hand, sending a cold breeze over my palm. "All right."

74

My head tilts on its side. "That easy? You're just going to let me change?"

"I'm not going to force you. But *I* won't be changing." He pinches the cotton material loosely hanging over his abs. "This is exactly the wardrobe the night calls for."

I purse my lips together, biting back a grin and a curse I'd like to drop on him. He's good at the reverse psychology—I consider changing for only a second before deciding to grab my purse and lock the door behind us. I shake my head at the victorious expression he's donning.

"The gloating smile isn't the most attractive thing," I lie through my teeth. He laughs, claiming my hand once more and swinging it between our bodies as we make our way to the passenger side of the truck. He gave it a good run with a hose, but I can tell he abandoned the idea of a professional wash with flecks of stubborn mud clinging to the underside of the door.

"So… are you going to remain mysterious?" I ask him after I buckle in and he starts up the engine. "Or do I get to know what it is we're doing?"

He presses his lips together thoughtfully. "I don't think I've *ever* been described as mysterious."

I drop my jaw in mock shock. "Really? But you're so reserved."

He chuckles and pulls the truck into gear, the muscles in his forearm flexing and teasing me in the sunset light.

"I unfortunately got called in to work tonight. I was hoping you would tagalong."

My shoulders slump in disappointment, brows pulling

inward. "You work in your pajamas?"

"Sometimes," he admits, giving me a side glance. "This particular meeting requires it."

I shake my head at him. More mystery. "You're enjoying this, aren't you?"

"There's a wrinkle right above your nose that is absolutely gorgeous. It seems to only pop up when I say something you aren't expecting." He grins and nods toward me. "Like right now, for instance."

Warmth creeps through my neck, and I quickly put a hand over the wrinkle. A girlish grin threatens on my lips, and I chase it away with a laugh and look out the window. "Have you been described as unpredictable?"

"That one I've heard *a lot*."

He takes us into the city, turning toward the cluster of office and news buildings, basically the hub of our community. My building used to be this far North until Garrison decided to move it closer to the suburban homes most of our clients find appealing. It's helpful for the commute—I spent double on gas at the other building. Now we're in a much more central location.

The sun ducks behind the mountain range we just left behind us, casting us in a soft blue light that, if possible, makes Cooper look even handsomer. The blue in his eyes seems to intensify just before he turns into a parking garage. He pulls into a spot reserved for him, *Cooper Sterling, Executive Parking* in reflective white paint on the cement wall.

He shuts the diesel engine off, instantly quieting the

garage.

"Here we are."

"Is this your office?" I ask, cranking the door open. His eyes flick to my hand before he holds a single finger up.

"Wait right there."

I let go of the handle, leaving the door open while he climbs out. He's tall enough that I can see his blond head bob around the truck, and I take a moment to admire the naturally highlighted strands. Most of my teenage bedroom was adorned in blond heartthrobs. I've always been drawn to the sun-kissed look, but have found it rare in the men I've come in contact with in reality.

He steps in front of my door, and I let go of my thoughts so they don't sneak their way off my tongue.

"May I?" he offers, gesturing to my waist.

My first thought is, *not a chance*. The cake I devoured the night before traveled to that exact spot, and I don't revel in the idea of him touching such squishy areas.

My eyes drift to his very sturdy-looking shoulders, and I end up deciding to hell with it. I swivel sideways and hook my palms atop his shoulders while he wraps his strong hands around my waist. He plucks me from my seat as if I weigh 100 pounds less than I actually do and ever-so-gently sets me on my feet next to his. I like it here—sharing body heat and feeling feminine and beautiful when I rarely feel this way. It weakens my ability to think, so I release my hold on his shoulders, and he reluctantly lets go of my waist.

"Thank you," he says, his breath warm and minty over my head.

"For…?"

He smirks. "That was more for me than it was for you."

His eyes drift up from my lips, and I push a hand over the nose wrinkle I hope I won't be hyper aware of now that he's pointed it out. I'll just have to learn to be perfectly unsurprised by him.

I let out a breath and take his hand, noticing the twitch in his dimple the moment I do. Perhaps that is his "nose wrinkle," and I intend to be as unpredictable as he is to test my theory.

He leads us past another executive spot, that one saying it's reserved for a Robert Sterling.

"Related?" I ask, nodding to the white paint. He follows my gaze and nods.

"My brother."

"Older? Younger?"

"Younger." He grins, stepping up to an elevator and inserting a key. "He's coming up on his thirtieth. I plan to make it as torturous for him as he did for me."

"What was so bad about yours?"

We step inside the private elevator, and Cooper sticks his key in again before hitting a button for one of the upper levels.

"Paid for company."

"Escort service?"

His head falls back as he laughs. "Not quite as scandalous. It was a just the moment I realized that my life wasn't all that I'd wanted it to be, especially when I had made no genuine connections to any other human being.

Not everyone can handle my social awkwardness." His eyes meet mine. "Very depressing day."

I think back to only a few days prior, to my own thirtieth. No paid for company, but I didn't exactly want company at all. It was a *fabulous* day.

"We really are such polar opposites," I tell him, looking up at the numbers ticking through the floors. "My thirtieth was the moment I realized my life was everything I wanted it to be."

"You spent it with friends? Family?"

"My cats."

He chuckles. "Just when I think you couldn't possibly be more captivating, you make even small talk something worth discussing."

Is this small talk? It feels deeper to me, like tiny sparks of light making who he is much clearer, but perhaps to someone like him, this is small. I find myself involuntarily inching closer to him, my cheek grazing the sleeve of his pajama shirt. I can feel the small amount of contact all the way into my toes.

The elevator hits the level we need, and the doors open to a very loud studio. There are so many people with headsets, clipboards, and cell phones running around a giant set of beds. My eyebrows rise, and I look up to Cooper and wait for him to explain exactly what I'm tagging along for.

He holds back a grin at my reluctance, nearly tugging me onto the studio floor.

"Cooper…" I say, eying the crew, all donning different versions of the same shirt we're wearing. He stops pulling and steps in front of me, reaching to swipe a loose strand of hair from my eyes, but stopping himself and letting his arm fall back to his side.

"You're not camera shy, are you?"

9

Meet the Sheets

Truth? I'm not camera shy. My face is on business cards and I'm not opposed to posting the occasional selfie with my cats.

However, when I'm faced with a professional commercial and advertising crew, I am incredibly camera shy.

My feet slide on the floor as I dig my heels into the smooth surface. "Cooper…"

"Relax." He squeezes my hand. "We're just the stand-ins."

"And what does that entail?"

"Mostly messing around in front of the camera while they test the lighting."

That doesn't sound horrible, but I tilt a skeptical eyebrow in his direction anyhow.

He lets out a light chuckle. "Come on, I'll show you."

I step into him, tucking close to his arm as busy crew members briskly walk around us. He leads me past one of the photo shoots, a bare-chested male model stealing my attention for half a second—or perhaps longer by the amused look Cooper gives me when I turn back to him.

"He's the actual clothing model," Cooper explains. "Probably the header of the ad campaign while this one"— He nods up ahead—"is the footnote."

A second camera crew is setting up around a giant, fluffy bed. The comforter is bright white, reminiscent of the bedding in the million dollar home I showed to him just yesterday. A rush of excitement overwhelms my stomach as Cooper pulls me right up to the queen-size.

"What exactly are you advertising?" I ask, tempted to run my fingers over the duvet.

"Sterling Advertising runs all the campaigns for Cozy King." He drops my hand and flops onto the bed. "Stand-in days are good ones."

My lips turn up, amused at the hand he's using to smooth and prepare the spot next to him for me. He waggles a playful brow, and biting back a laugh, I turn and fall backward into the soft comfort of a memory foam mattress and must-be Egyptian cotton material.

"I could live right here," I say with a sigh, staring up at the rafters in the incomplete ceiling.

"You can." The sheets shift as he tucks his hands under his head. "Well, until the director of photography shows up."

I run my hands over the comforter, electricity shocking up my knuckles when they accidentally bump into his hip. I haven't bought myself a birthday present yet; maybe I'll give the Cozy King a few of my hard-earned dollar bills… if they have any sheets in a brighter color.

"This is what I picture," Cooper muses, keeping his eyes on the rafters above us. "Five years from now, I want to fall back onto a bed after a long day and just lie there in silence with a beautiful woman."

"You can lie in silence alone," I counter with a smart tilt of my lips. "Don't have to share the comforter either."

His stomach shakes with quiet laughter. "Solitude doesn't quite do it for me."

A prick of pain hollows out something I've kept deep inside for a long time. I understand the feeling; I'm unfortunately all too familiar with it. My best friend was married when I was twenty. My sister found love when I was twenty-three. My brother followed soon after that. There were several years I spent wallowing in what I thought wasn't fair, and I often fretted over what was wrong with me. Where was the man I was meant to spend my life with? Start a family? As time went on, my friends and family grew in their own families, I found solace and comfort in the fact that I was able to do *so much* on my own. I didn't have to be lonely—I had me, and that was enough. That *is* enough.

Besides, I've seen what a family turns into—the hellion two-year-olds and early dinner dates. Overbearing husbands who don't allow you to eat cake and too many mouths to feed and not enough money to feed them. I internally scoff at the idea of actually *wanting* to have that. I was clearly a clueless twenty-something.

"I'm scaring you again," Cooper says, turning his head

toward me.

"No." I face him. "It's just rare to meet a man with his head so up in the clouds. I never know how to respond."

"So far it's been with carefully placed wit." The whites of his teeth tease me in his smile, the blues of his eyes studying every wrinkle in my expression. I know he's teasing, flirting, playing the game that everyone plays on a first date, though this version is definitely different than what I'm used to. Yet, his words are running straight to my heart; sarcasm can only get our conversation so far, and if I'm never as straight with him as he has been with me, we'll be playing the game a lot longer than we should.

The flirt and playfulness in my smile dissipates, and his brow furrows slightly before his gaze flicks to just over my shoulder.

"Son of a… What are you doing here?"

I twist to see who he's looking at—a man with dirty blond hair and a clean shaven face. He matches Cooper in height, or at least has to be close. Running from just behind his right ear down the curve of his neck and disappearing into his collared button-down is a jagged scar that immediately after noticing, I try my hardest not to stare at.

The man tilts his head slightly to the side, lifting a to-go cup to his lips. "Guess my schedule opened up."

The bed shifts behind me as Cooper pushes from it. "Could've called." He makes an obvious gesture with is eyes toward me before extending his hand to help me up.

He shrugs. "Lost my phone."

Cooper rolls a pair of exasperated eyes that land on me,

and I feel as if I should understand the irritation, but I'm not quite caught up yet.

"Maya, this is my brother Robbie."

"Ah," I say with a knowing grin. "The annoyance makes sense now."

Robbie laughs, pointing at Cooper with his cup. "He's pissing a fit 'cause one of us had to supervise the shoot."

"And you insisted your plans were unbreakable, as were mine."

Robbie shakes his head and swallows. "No… you said your plans were *flexible*." His eyes move to me. "Looks like it's going just fine. She's still here, isn't she?"

Cooper weaves his fingers with mine, and I have to bite away a twitterpated grin when the deep blues of his eyes lock onto me. "That she is."

There must be a silence long enough to make Robbie feel like he has to clear his throat to get our attention back, but it sure doesn't feel like it was nearly enough time.

"So… big bro, you two stand in for the next ten minutes then you can scamper off while I supervise the rest of this very exciting bedding ad. Good with you?"

Cooper turns to me. "Good with *you*?"

"Will there be food at some point this evening?" I ask, starting to wonder if I should've eaten before he picked me up.

"Right after this."

"Then that plan is *great* with me."

Robbie's gaze distinctly moves down my frame, his lips curling upward, and I self-consciously wonder if he's amused

85

by the fact that a fuller body type wants a trip to the trough, but I quickly shake it from my head. I shouldn't worry about the approval of Cooper's family members—there is no reason for it now or ever. I snicker to myself at the fact that my mind went there all on its own.

"We're ready, Mr. Sterling," a girl with a headset and clipboard says, looking at Cooper, but it's Robbie who answers.

"Great. Maya, you want to climb up on the bed? Grab a pillow, will ya?"

I give Cooper a hesitant glance, and he grins and reaches across the mattress for one of the well-fluffed pillows. He playfully tosses it in my direction, and a squeak of surprise floats from my mouth.

"Watch it, buddy," I tease, then trip my way up onto the bed. Robbie tells me to stay standing, keeping the pillow above my head while he directs Cooper to position himself flat on his back between my legs. A rare blush tints Cooper's ears as he follows the direction, causing my mouth to turn up and soft giggles to erupt from somewhere deep in my abdomen.

"Perfect," Robbie says, and the evil glint in his expression tells me that he's enjoying embarrassing his brother a little too much. Cooper may be overly forward with his words, but his touch has been nothing but slow, sweet, and cautious ever since he apologized for kissing me on his run. I can tell the comfortable position for him right now would be to hold onto my ankle or run his hand up my leg, but since that's a level we haven't progressed to, he's

86

awkwardly stretching his arms to the side. I hold back a laugh as I stare down at him.

"This is so very tempting," I say, giving the pillow a little squeeze. "One swift move and I'll ruin that great hair you've got going for you tonight."

My light-heartedness seems to relax him, his body loosening enough that he doesn't look so frigid on the very comfortable mattress.

"I think that was his intention." He nods toward his brother who is now directing me to angle my hips toward the camera. I rock a little on the bed, and whether out of instinct or just a genuine reflex, Cooper grabs hold just under the back of my knee. The soft touch sends my head spinning, and though I know he's helping me keep my balance, I have to breathe a few times to keep from falling on top of him.

"Whoa there," he says through a laugh. I get my footing and reposition myself to where Robbie wants me. The pressure Cooper's putting on my leg starts to wane, his hesitancy creasing the lines near his mouth.

"You should keep your hand there," I reassure him.

A noticeable air of relief passes in his eyes. "I like the way you think."

He flexes, his fingers tickling enough to get a giggle out of me but not enough for me to lose my balance. Robbie tells me to bring the pillow down in front so they can see how the lighting is on my face. I try to follow the instructions, but Cooper's starting to make faces at me, and it's mighty distracting.

"I thought you were a professional," I tease him as he does a blowfish impression. It's incredibly sexy on him.

"Who told you that?"

I laugh and let the pillow swing down and flump against the side of his face. When his eyes open, I lift one shoulder and say, "Sorry."

"You're gonna be."

"I wasn't talking to you." I glance over my shoulder at Robbie from behind the camera. "Sorry!" I say louder. "It slipped."

Cooper's fingers grow relentless in their tickling, and I curl in laughter, dropping on top of his stomach.

He lets out a whoosh of breath, and I hold mine while I wait for his to come back. I forgot that I'm not the lightest person in the world—with him teasing me and looking at me like I'm the actual model in front of this camera, I felt like a size two.

"Oh, hold it there," Robbie says. Cooper's head whips around in a panic, and a similar feeling drops a weight into my gut. I shift on him, trying to hold most of my weight on my knees and less on him. His hands make a quick trip from my legs to my waist.

"Uh… you may want to hold still."

Warmth spreads over my cheeks. "Sorry," I say, genuinely this time. "I don't want to crush you."

His brows pull in. "You're not."

"I can see it on your face, liar." I laugh. "This is really not comfortable for you."

His eyes soften before they move past me and to the

ceiling. "Maya… you're straddling me on a bed, and I'm in pajama bottoms. Trust me, the problem is that I'm *too* comfortable."

The realization hits, and a bubble of laughter rises up inside me. I let it out and wiggle on top of him, laughing when I find that he's very much telling the truth.

He reaches above his head for another pillow, and I whack him with mine before he can get a shot in. Robbie lets us toss around, the flashes of the camera going off only barely registering in my brain. If I had to take a guess, I'd bet that I'll never be asked to play stand-in again.

***

"How much do I owe you?" I ask Cooper, waving the 5x7 print at him as we head back to his truck. When Robbie went through the test film, I saw one shot that I just had to own. The rest were okay, too, but I doubt I'll be seeing my face in any bedding ad.

Cooper grins and plucks it from my fingers, sliding it nicely into a protective sheet. "Consider it payment for the session."

I chuckle. "Yes, that sounds fair for the *incredible* job I did."

He shakes his head, letting his eyes drift over the photo. "Why this one?" he asks before handing it over.

"You kidding? Check out my ass. I can't believe it isn't photo-shopped."

"Let the record show that I have permission from this moment forward to check out Maya Baker's ass." He sets his hands on my hips, sends a flock of fluttering wings through my chest, and spins me around to get a better look at the real thing. I should tell him the real reason I want the photo—his smile is absolutely killer in it.

I playfully tap at his hands to get him to let me go, but his fingers weave with mine, and I can feel his chest inch closer to my back. It makes it difficult to walk, but I don't mind it one bit.

"Can I boldly assume this is going well?" he asks, holding up our joined hands.

"You can," I tell him, "but if you don't feed me soon, I will reconsider."

He momentarily turns off all brain activity as he presses his lips softly against the nape of my neck. I have to find the air around us as the world tilts on its axis, my feet tingle in my flip-flops, and my tongue is in danger of putting a voice to my unholy thoughts.

The sudden brightness of the truck's headlights as Cooper disarms it shines some sense into me.

"You okay with pizza?" he asks, putting some mind-clearing space between our bodies to open the door for me. My gaze floats up to his happy and hopeful eyes.

Damn it... that look is the kicker, isn't it? It's the face of someone who hopes this is going somewhere beyond a few fun dates (and hopefully a few frisky nights.) A giant cloud settles over my head, threatening to pour hateful insults all over me—phrases and names that would describe me if I wasn't completely frank about my intentions right now.

"I won't fall in love with you."

The tilting world drops to its knees, swaying Cooper on

the spot. For once, I'm throwing *him* for a loop.

His strong hand flexes on the door handle, the tendons rising under his skin all the way up his forearm. His brow wrinkles in slight amusement, and he lets out a small laugh along with his words. "I'm not as quick with the wit as you are, so you'll have to forgive this." He circles a finger at his adorably stunned expression, making what I have to say that much harder.

"You've been very clear on your intentions," I explain, toying with the edge of the photo in my hands. "I'm making sure you're clear on mine."

He presses his lips together, and even that creases the lines in his cheek that completely drive me to the brink of insanity.

"That's fair." He settles against the truck door, letting me have the floor. Now that I have it, I have to gather my thoughts so they come out the right way. I've never had this conversation—never a need for it—so I don't know where to start.

"I don't want marriage," I say, opting to just go for it. "I don't want kids. I don't want that life you described, the life *you* want."

He stands in thoughtful patience, taking in every word that falls from my lips as if they were something precious. It throws me off a bit, and I find my mind fumbling around for explanations.

"Life is *really* good right now. I've got my own place, I live for myself, I have freedom and possibilities… I enjoy the fun parts of relationships." I wave a finger between us.

"These parts. First dates, first touches, first kisses. After a while they become stale and unfeeling. I don't want to venture into that territory... So while this is going well, and I too find you *insanely* attractive, this won't be going anywhere."

The storm cloud over my head starts to clear, creating an overcast forecast. I feel better, but I also feel a sense of loss at the same time. If only we were looking for the same things, whether it's both of us wanting something serious or both of us wanting something fun, then I wouldn't have felt this obligation to bring this up and put such a sour taste on an otherwise perfect evening.

He tilts his head, studying my jittery movements. "Why agree to go out with me at all?" he asks, his voice light.

"Curiosity, mostly." I shrug. "You also caught me in a weak moment."

His brow pulls in briefly before the memory returns to him. A wicked glint flickers in the deep blues of his eyes, and he shoves from the car door and closes the distance between us. His strong fingers run through my hair and grip at the back of my head, stealing the breath from my lungs. His lips come down on mine, anxious and hungry, erasing any confusion settling in the corners of my mind.

"Go out with me again." His request comes out in a breathless grunt between our lips. I can't seem to string two thoughts together. The stars have been plucked from the sky and placed behind my eyes, and the thought of saying no seems ludicrous; why would I ever turn away the possibility of another moment like this one?

"You are evil," I tell him with a grin, catching onto his game.

"Is that a yes?"

"It won't change my mind."

He taps a kiss to my nose and steps back, the smile lines creasing his cheeks. "I like you, Maya. I'm not looking to change your mind. I want to know what's inside of it."

10

Agree to Disagree

This place is ginormous. I feel like an itty bitty ant as I stretch up to ring the bell. I half expect a tuxedo-donning butler to answer the big wooden door and offer to take my coat... well, if I were wearing one.

When Cooper sent me the address and told me to come over ready to eat, I waited a full hour before agreeing. I hardly ever say yes to second dates—mostly because I rarely get asked on them—but Cooper has discovered the key to my stubbornness, and it's not just his kissing skills.

I do a quick check of the ladies to make sure they're not popping out of the deeply cut, heart-shaped bodice of my only little black dress. It's been a while since I pulled this number out, the last guy I thought worthy of it I dated when I was twenty-six. It's a little tight around the middle, but I think it'll still do the trick.

The lock on the door clicks, and my stomach flutters up to the sky, pulling the corners of my mouth with it on the trip. Cooper greets my clown-ish grin with one of his own, his eyes staying on mine for a good three seconds before taking a detour up and down my dress. I do a slow spin for him just for fun.

"You approve?"

"Hang on." He braces himself using the doorframe. "Trying to find the right word."

"That bad?"

"You're gorgeous." His foot falls onto the porch as he takes a step toward me, and I glance down just enough to notice he's barefoot. "It's good to see you."

My gaze roams over his face, down to his shoulders and chest that's covered in a deep blue, long-sleeved Henley, his muscular forearms peeking out from the rolled up sleeves. He's in a pair of khaki cargos that hug him quite nicely, a pen hooked onto one of the side pockets. I'm in danger of throwing myself at him; khakis are my weakness, and I'd never ever admit that to anyone, even my cats.

"Likewise," I say, wishing that my breathless voice sounded more flirty than it did flighty, but by the look on his face, he seems to like getting me all hot and bothered.

"Hungry?"

"Starving."

He slides his fingers between mine, leads me inside the mansion, and grins wide at the gasp that slips through my teeth.

I'm a realtor; I've seen million dollar homes and foreclosed P.O.S.'s. I've seen everything from horribly painted walls and half-eaten carpets to marble staircases and ten-thousand dollar rugs. When you see a house like the outside of this one, there's an expectation of the inside. This one defies them all.

"Surprised?"

"You could say that," I tell him with a laugh, glancing around at the very… well, there's no other way to describe it… *family-esk* décor. To our left is a parlor area, but it looks more like a playroom for a daycare. Toys in colorful buckets on organized shelves, one wall painted in chalkboard paint, drawings of stick figures and undefined swirls faded as if they tried to erase them, but they had a faulty eraser.

To our right is the dining and kitchen area, both of those looking more like what I'd expect from a million-dollar home, except in place of a dining room table, a checkered picnic blanket is spread across the fluffy carpet. Battery-operated tea lights line the edges, a couple of plates covered with sterling silver lids sit on either side, and a bucket with a bottle of champagne rests just off the blanket.

"Aww," I say, slipping my shoes off, grateful that he's decided to go casual for the night. "You cooked?"

"I'm trying to impress you… so no. I left the cooking to the professionals." He laughs. "At least for now. Home cooking will be on date five."

"Ambitious." I take my spot on the pillow soft blanket, tucking my legs under me and controlling the relaxing moan in the back of my throat. "What makes you so sure we'll get to a date five?"

"I'm never sure of anything," he says as he sits, the rustle of his pants drawing my attention to his legs, his upper thighs, his crotch. I blink myself back up to his face before he calls me out on it, because heaven knows that he would. "I live on a hope and a prayer."

"I wouldn't even know what that looks like," I admit. I have dreams and hopes, but they're always grounded in reality.

He gives me a look that tells me that he's more interested in that comment than he's letting on, but he's keeping his thoughts to himself for once. My teeth slide over my bottom lip, and I reach for the lid to my dish.

"Hang on," he says, putting a hand on top of the sterling silver. "Sea food or beef?"

"What if I'm a vegetarian?"

"Considering you downed bacon strips in under a minute and inhaled a slice of meat lover's, I ruled a vegetarian dish out."

"I love how you describe how I eat," I say, trying to hide my self-consciousness over the fact that he's one hundred percent right. "Maybe I'll bulldoze through this meal, too."

"Please do," he says on a sigh. "It's sexy as hell."

A snort billows from my nose, and I push his hand off the lid. "I'll eat whatever you put in front of me," I say, lifting it up from the plate. Steam rises up from the beautifully cooked lobster, a bed of broccoli and rice as a side, and of course, melted butter to dip. He definitely ordered out, and he ordered out nicely.

"Not trading," I tell him through a mouthful of drool.

"Good." He laughs and lifts his own lid, a juicy, thick burger in front of him, a side of fries and dipping sauce to the side. I tilt an eyebrow, curious over the two choices.

"Is there a reason we aren't eating the same thing?"

"Yes." His eyebrows waggle as he hands me a lobster bib. "I'm running an experiment."

"Do I get to know the details?"

"No," he says with a grin. "But I'll let you know the results. So far, they're going pretty well."

Well, no better way to put pressure on me while I eat. I'm about to tell him that, but he redirects my mind when he pulls out a couple of beers and pops the tops. I'm not much of a beer drinker, but I take it anyway. Maybe if I pass whatever experiment he's doing, he'll pop open that champagne.

"You want the bubbly, don't you?" he asks, and I widen my eyes and shake my head.

"I'm fine."

"Don't lie."

I guess I can't with him. Maybe I'm an open book, too.

My shoulders fall and I pick up my glass flute and stick it out, offering up a cheesy grin. He laughs and pushes up to his knees. I get the best view of his ass, the ice in the bucket shifting as he pulls out the champagne bottle. I tie my bib around my neck and get ready to chomp down on my food.

"Question…" I say around my first delectable bite. "Why in the hell do you want to move? This place seems pretty perfect for you already."

He shakes his head, tipping the flute so the champagne doesn't stain the blanket. "Oh this isn't mine. A buddy is letting me crash at his place while he's on vacation."

"Are all your buddies billionaires?" I ask, taking the drink from him and watching as he digs into his own food.

"Just this one. And my brother."

I get a round of flutters at the fact that he considers his brother his buddy. "Is that why you don't act like the typical…" My thumb goes to the tip of my nose and I push it high in the air to imitate the snob nob people I usually encounter when selling high-dollar homes. Cooper snorts his beer right through his nose. He coughs and sputters, grappling for a napkin while he tries to compose himself.

"You're gonna kill me before dessert," he says, his voice strained before he takes another sip of beer that goes down the right pipe. I giggle and take my tenth or so bite of lobster and fifth scoop of rice. Wow… maybe I do need to slow down. Cooper hasn't even touched his fries yet, and if he doesn't hurry, I'll find my way over to those, too.

He clears his throat, and he blows out a breath, his composure back now. "I wish I had a good answer for ya," he says, plucking up a fry and swirling it in the sauce. "Maybe because I know how lucky I am. Or maybe because I know numbers and I know if I'm not careful, I could lose everything. Or maybe because I have to keep working for it every day." He pauses for a second, his eyes playfully teasing me. I rub at my chin, butter running down my finger as I swipe it away. "Or maybe I'm just awesome."

"That *has* to be it." I grab a napkin and try to clean myself up. I don't know what's wrong with me; I am a first date expert. I've gone out for food hundreds of times and managed to not stuff myself or go to fast, but with Cooper…

he makes it so easy to let loose.

"I have a question for you now," he says, his eyes carefully placed on my butter-covered lobster bib before he brings them up to me.

"Listening…"

"You said something last night that… well, it stuck out to me, and I was just curious about it."

Oh he's going to have to be more specific. "What'd I say?"

"Something about how you think all relationships inevitably turn stale."

"You really do avoid any ounce of small talk." I lick the end of my fork, the tines pressing into my bottom lip as I shake my head. "You just dive right into the deep end of the pool."

"Is it because all your relationships turned stale? Or was it someone else's?"

I press my lips together, biting away the smile I have that he's not falling for my attempt at a subject change. "Both, I guess." I take a sip of bubbly, letting the alcohol relax me and the carbonation get me giddy enough to have this conversation without getting defensive. It's not his fault; he has a right to know why I don't want marriage or kids, and he has no clue that I get those questions all the time. "Why don't you want a fling? Too many women? Time to settle down?"

He nearly chokes on his beer again. "Um… no. There've been others, but I'm not much of a one-time kind of guy."

100

"And I'm not a long-term kind of girl." I brush my hair from my face, feeling a little warm now that the alcohol is sinking in. "The good stuff is in the 'firsts.' First glance, first touch, first kiss. First date, first night over, first orgasm. Seconds aren't bad when it was so good the first time." I take another sip of champagne, adding that last part in so he knows just how great it's been so far with him. I'd probably take third and fourth and fifth helpings before we finally get sick of each other.

I set my empty flute down, smacking my wetted lips. "So yes, I'm having fun with you now. That first date of ours was the best date I've been on in… Okay, best date I've *ever* been on. And my god, the way you kiss me, Cooper. My toes curl, I swear it."

He lets out a laugh, and I feel my cheeks warming at how loose my tongue is getting. I let out a long sigh that rumbles my lips. "But it won't last. This… intense feeling that I get in my stomach? It's only because this is new. It'll disappear after we learn all there is to know about each other. When there are no more surprises."

"You really believe it'll get boring? You'll have nothing left to talk about?"

I lift a shoulder and put my fork down. "After a few months there isn't anything left to learn. That's not just from personal experience. That's common knowledge."

"No." He shakes his head hard. "No, I don't believe that for a second. A year, ten years, fifty… there is always going to be something to say, something to learn about the person you love."

I slowly shake my head, dropping my gaze to my empty plate. "I just don't think like that. Even this"—I wave my finger between the two of us—"will burn out. Especially if you're diving into the deep stuff right in the beginning."

He tilts his head, his back straightening like a shock went right up his spine. His lips kink up, his brow pulls down, and he looks completely bewildered by that statement, like I'd just spouted it in Greek.

"Stay with me," he blurts, and I blink a few times to make sure I heard him right and I'm not overly buzzed.

"What was that?"

"I'll be here for a while," he says with a nod at the mansion he's staying at. "Take two weeks, spend them here with me. I'll prove to you that things can be just as exciting as they are in the beginning."

"How exactly would staying with you do that?"

"Pretend we're not on date number three right now."

"This is date number two."

"I'm counting brunch." He playfully wrinkles his nose at me. "And it's a moot point anyway. Because let's just, pretend we're twelve months into this thing."

"A year."

"You ever made it a year before?"

I run a tongue over my lips, the dryness of them probably caused by my rapid breathing and the fact that I can't keep my jaw closed during this conversation. Do I really want to admit to him that I haven't had a relationship last longer than three months? And that was so long ago, I barely remember it. Fun and flirt is my forte. When it's no longer either of those things, I duck out, or he does. Singlehood suits me.

"All right. Here it is…" he says, relieving me from answering his previous question. He closes the gap between us, taking my hand in his. "I like you. I want to really get to know you. And I plan on asking you out again. And again. And again and again. But if you think it's not gonna go past all the firsts, let's just… fast forward. See if you can handle a relationship that's in a year deep. Then we'll know."

He's off his rocker. He's a bona fide dreamer, his head so up in the clouds that I can't even see it from where I stand, my two feet rooted into the soft earth. I can't stay with him; he'd see me when I wake up with no makeup, maybe catch me after having one of my late night snacks, crippled over with indigestion. And if we're truly going to pretend that we've been in a relationship for a year, maybe even *married*, will we talk? Will we go out? Do I need to dress it up or keep it casual? What are the rules, here? I've always ducked out before it ever got to the point of passing gas in front of each other and passing out in the bed after a long day without even touching. How in the world can that be better than the dolling up, getting spoiled out on the town, the butterflies in the stomach, and the sexual tension in the air?

Wait… does that mean sex isn't even in the near future? Because I have a problem with that.

"Is this… I mean, is this another experiment? Trying to test me out to see if I'm marriage material? Because I'll tell you right now that I'm not."

He drops his blond head, and I see his shoulder blades shaking with laughter. "If you want to think of it as an experiment, that's fine. But it's not about seeing if you're marriage material." He lifts his eyes. "If anything, I'd like to convince you to take a chance on *me*."

I'm already taking a chance on him. Believe me, if he wasn't so unique and interesting and surprising, I would've stopped us in our tracks the second I found out we wanted different things. But as I watch his thoughts roll around behind his eyes, listen to his breathing as he waits for my thoughts about this, I have to admit, he could be worth it. He already said he'd ask me out again, and I'll say yes; I know I will. I'll say yes to every time the question falls from his lips until the day we lose this electric spark. And I have a strong feeling that Cooper Sterling could be the guy who could rip my heart out if I let him anywhere near it. Maybe it's a smart move to find out now while my heart is still solely mine.

"How do you do that?" I ask, narrowing my eyes and shaking my head at him. "How do you make such insane ideas sound…"

"Fun?" he offers, hope rising up in his expression.

"Logical."

"Well," he says, nodding to my empty glass. "The alcohol probably helped a little."

"I don't know." I let out a breathless laugh. "I'm pretty sure you sobered me up, and I still think that you have a point."

"Is that a yes?"

I tug at the hem of my dress, not ready to give him a yes or a no. "It's an 'I'll sleep on it.'"

His mouth pulls into a slow smile, one that will weaken my every resolve if he keeps it up much longer. He claps his hands free from his food and starts to rise from the blanket. "Okay, let me give you the tour."

"It's not a yes, Cooper." *Yet.*

"I know… but I figure showing off my buddy's mansion could help nudge you off that fence you're on."

He holds his hand out for me, and after giving him a good long look, I take it. Maybe seeing more playrooms will help remind me that we are so not made for each other, and he'll be easier to say no to, even though the tingles in my fingers from being in contact with his big, warm hands tell me otherwise.

11

Wack Verbal Contract

I pull at the knot in my tankini, trying to get it untangled before I toss it into a suitcase to join a pile of various wardrobe choices. A few minutes into my struggling, I slump onto the bed and fling it toward my dresser.

"I can't do this," I mutter for the third time since I've started packing. I took all night to sleep on it, all day at work to think about it, and still my head keeps teetering from one decision to the other. I'm half convinced that taking Cooper's offer is a good idea, half convinced I have lost my mind.

All I want is to spend some time with the man. He's attractive and handsome and *seriously, the kissing…* It's my Achilles heel. As much as I try to talk myself into turning down his every advance, putting it into practice is so much harder.

I turn to Tom, who is curled up in the empty space of my suitcase, and scratch his black and white head. "It's more about the house than the guy," I tell him, falling to the low point of convincing my cat why staying with Cooper would be a good idea. "You should see this place, Tom. Indoor pool, private balcony, open bar… any girl would *die* for a week like this."

I don't mention the company the vacation also provides because I'm determined to let my decision be Cooper-influence free. But if I were to mention it, it'd definitely be added to the pros column.

Tom leans his head into my hand and purrs so loudly I bet Kat will be in here any second to try to get in on the back rub. I let out a sigh and rest my head on the unorganized mess I plan on taking with me, if I decide to go. The main problem still exists, though; he wants to show me what married life would be like, but he doesn't *know* what it will be like. I don't either, for that matter. I only know what I see, and he only knows what he's seen. Our perception on the subject is so far off from one another, and I don't see either of us changing our minds. I'd hate to indulge in the newness of what I can already feel is an exciting and addicting infatuation, only to get to the inevitable boredom a few months later. He may want that boredom, find excitement in something long term and promising. He wants a wife, a family, a settled life… things I don't ever see for myself.

It's dangerous and completely unfair. I know it is. I feel as if I've already gone down the road farther than I should have. Every time I talk myself into walking away, I see his smile, picture that dimple. I hear his laugh and wish he were near so I could tease and flirt my way into his head, because he sure as hell is in mine.

"Who am I kidding?" I say to my chubby cat. "This is so about the man."

I pluck Tom from the suitcase and dump all the clothing at the foot of my bed. I'm stuffing this thing into the darkest corner of my closet where it can't be found.

What I need is a little reminder of why I'm so set in my ways. I flick on Siri and ask her where the nearest club is. Having a night to innocently flirt with men who are just looking for a non-committal romp is the prescription I need for my Cooper addiction.

I'm not one to go off without my wingman, however, so before dedicating to the evening, I should send a message to Holland to see if she's okay coming. It may not be the most fun place for an expectant mother, but my other choices require babysitters on short notice.

I trip over the pile of clothing I just spread all over my floor and bounce across my bed to get to my phone plugged in the charger. Just as I get a grip on it, Kat leaps up on my nightstand and jolts me backward. That kitten must get her skittish tendencies from her owner.

"Shush," I tell them, even though my cats rarely mewl during my phone calls. Rolling to my back, I hold my phone over my head and swipe the screen on.

Cooper, 1 new message

Forgetting why I needed my phone in the first place, I open up the message, heart pounding as if my teenage self was in the company of Nick Carter.

Thought you looked really beautiful in this one.

Attached is one of the photos from the shoot, but not one from the test shots. Robbie, or someone else on set, must've taken it while I was hyena laughing at something that evening. Could've been from a number of moments, if I'm being honest. My mouth is split open in unabashed amusement, eyes crinkled in the corners and smile lines creasing near my mouth. I reach up and smooth over my cheek, frowning at how *old* I'm starting to look. I can feel my nose wrinkled in disgust as I type back a simple, Ugh. Aging may suit Cooper well—*very well*—but I am not pulling it off.

I scoot my way off my mattress and pad across the carpet to the adjoining bathroom. I think there is some eye cream in here somewhere; a few years ago, I got cornered at the mall by one of those pushy salesmen and ended up with two hundred dollars' worth of anti-aging cream. Julie still hasn't let me live that one down.

After a few minutes of digging around under my sink, my phone vibrates across the counter. My heart gets another round of Nick Carter-like beats.

Unacceptable response ;)

I shake my head and type back, *You'll delete that photo if you know what's good for ya.*

You want to see a delete-worthy photo?

Before I can respond with a yes or no, the incoming attachment uploads. It's a close-up shot of just Cooper's nose and left eye. I laugh to myself, scaring my skittish orange kitten under the bed.

They really captured your boss-like essence. ;)

I'm relieved I had the brains to trim that day.

I give the shot another glance, my brow furrowing at the facial hair above his lip. *That is trimmed?*

I meant my nose hair. Then another picture comes in, his eyes wide in a goofy selfie. He's sitting in his bed right now, lying across it the way I'm sprawled across mine. My cheeks start to hurt from the all the smiling I've been doing during the conversation. Even when he's being a total goof, he's one of the most attractive specimens on the planet. Maybe even more-so.

I save the picture before typing back to him.

Can I bring my cats?

I hover over the send button, heart thumping through my chest, around my stomach, up into my throat, and then finally into my head where it makes me temporarily hard of hearing. My thumb presses the button, and I don't think I breathe for the twenty-two-and-a-half seconds it takes for him to respond.

Am I hearing a yes now?

If text messages had a tone, I would assume his was full of hope. Mine however would be a trembled mess, so I'm grateful that texts have yet to advance to that level of technology.

If I can bring my cats.

I send that one quickly before I can backtrack. I'm really doing this. I'm negotiating a verbal contract to be "married" to him for a couple of weeks. My hand flies up to cover my face, the realization hitting me so strongly I feel the need to make a few more conditions.

And I want my own room, I type before he has a chance to respond. *This isn't a romantic getaway. It's just an unorthodox way of proving to you that I'm right. If there is any shenanigans to be had, it won't involve me falling in love with you.*

It's only a few more seconds before my phone buzzes again, but it feels like a lifetime.

Got it.

Then another lifetime after that.

For the sake of clarity, I in no way promise not to fall in love with you.

I turn slowly from my bathroom, staring at his text as I plop back down on the bed. Finally, we're at the crossroad, moving forward with this ridiculous charade even though we both know how it'll end, or I can just end it now with one simple "no."

Tom nudges my elbow until I give in and scratch his head. "He won't fall in love with me," I say to my older and grumpier cat. It's the truth—after a full two weeks of uncensored Maya, any man, even one as quirky as Cooper, would turn around running. Perhaps all this will end in is a fun vacation in a mansion and an entertaining story for future girl's nights.

Yes, I believe I've thoroughly convinced myself. I give Tom a firm nod and straighten my spine as I type back.

Cooper Sterling, I accept.

12

Round and Wound

"Jim, I can't," I grunt out as the wheels on my suitcase get caught on the door jam. Tom's claws dig into my shoulder as I juggle him, my luggage, and my phone all at once.

"I'll pay you," my brother says over the line, his voice drowning in desperation. "Katie *needs* a day off."

"Then why don't…" I pause to mouth a thank you to Cooper who has magically appeared in the doorway to help me out. "Why don't you watch them and give her a spa day?"

A frustrated growl mixed with an impatient sigh fuzzes over the phone, and if my cat wasn't giving me a few new piercings, I'd probably laugh at whatever sound my brother just made.

"Look, it's been… a while. Between two hour intervals of feeding the baby and potty training the devil spawn, along with the fact that it was kicked off with a very *long* six weeks celibate, both of us could use a break *together*."

Wow. He must be really desperate if he's being so open

about his sex life. While my sister spouts off her bedroom secrets as if they're common knowledge, my brother tends to keep those things to himself. Thankfully.

My eyes flick up to Cooper patiently waiting for me to end the call. He offers up a grin, though the look in his eyes as they pass over my cats tells me he's not exactly thrilled with my plus-twos.

"Jim, I would. Trust me, I would watch your kids in a heartbeat, but I'm house-sitting with a…" I drift off, amusement raising my eyebrow as Cooper wildly waves to get my attention.

"It's okay," he mouths. My head tilts as I study his expression, wondering if it's genuine excitement resonating in his grin over *babysitting* or if he's just being nice. I'm assuming the former with his kid obsession.

"Maya?" Jim says, pulling my attention back into the conversation. I let out a sigh, giving in to the two men who completely ganged up on me.

"Are you okay with dropping them off?"

"Yes, yes," he says, and I can actually hear the smile I've put on his face. "Katie and I will probably just stay in anyway. Clean the house."

Sure. "I'll text you the address."

"Thank you, thank you, Maya."

I swipe the red button on my phone to end the call, shaking my head at the screen. "So much for using you as my ticket out of that one."

Cooper grins, pushing up off the suitcase he was leaning on. "How old are they?"

113

"Almost two months and just over two years." I snort, tucking my phone into the band of my yoga pants. One day they'll put pockets in these things. "You're in for it with that toddler. Even her father just called her 'devil spawn.' I couldn't disagree with him."

The smile that spreads across his face is equal to that of my devil spawned niece when she found the stash of Halloween candy two weeks early. "I can't wait."

"You're a very strange man, Cooper Sterling."

"Thank you." He grips the handle of my suitcase and lifts it up onto his shoulder. I gulp back a squeak of surprise... and arousal. That bag would never make it past checking with how many shoes I packed in it. "Which room do you desire, Miss Baker?"

"The big one," I joke. I hardly expect the master suite, but Cooper gives me one sharp nod and starts charging up the stairwell before I can give him a serious answer.

I grapple for Kat's carrier and make sure I have a good grip on Tom before following Cooper up. He's definitely in better shape than I am, not that I've done much to compete with him in that arena. If I were to lift anything, it would sooner be a forkful of cake than a barbell—though carrying my very obese cat up all these stairs should count for something.

"I was... not really being... serious—" My voice cuts off in the middle of my labored breathing. While the extravagant room is worth a shocked reaction, it's not the decor that I can't take my eyes off of. Cooper sets my luggage down, the muscles in his arms chorded with the

114

physical exertion. The moon streams in from the window, lighting up the handsome and knee-weakening features of his face—the boyish grin, the trimmed scruff, and the oceanic blue eyes. The reality of staying with such a tempting man hits me hard in the stomach, knocking the wind straight out of me. Heat fills me up from the inside out, dousing me in unexpected flames. I'm surprised I don't drop the cats and jump directly into his arms.

I knew this week would test my self-control, but I didn't realize it'd be immediately after I crossed the threshold.

"You sure?" Cooper teases.

"Huh?"

"You want another room?"

I nearly spit out that I'd like whatever room he's standing in, but I manage to keep that to myself.

Tom leaps from my arms and onto the king size bed, making himself right at home. Kat mewls from her carrier, scratching at the metal on the door. I set her down and let her out, and she starts clawing at the first pillow she can find.

"Unless *you'd* rather room with them?" I nod to my fur babies who have clearly already set up camp.

"Enjoy the master suite," Cooper quickly says, taking an exaggerated step around the bed to avoid the kitties. I press my lips together, shoving back the temptation to pick up either one of them and push them into Cooper's arms. If I did that, there's a good chance he'll be shoving a poopy two-year-old in mine when we watch my niece in a few days.

Cooper brushes past me, running a hand down my arm

in the process. A chill tingles up my spine, stealing away my thoughts for a moment.

"You tired?" he asks.

"Uh… uh huh." Well, I was. I should be. It's getting late, and I have an early day tomorrow. Yet here I stand, wide awake and hoping he gives in to the desire to touch me again.

"'Kay," he says, and I search for any ounce of disappointment in his expression. "So you know, because we're playing house, food is yours, pool is open, wander around… pig out and enjoy yourself."

"How romantic." I tilt my head. "Do I get to do any of these activities with you?"

He wrinkles his nose at me. "Not if you don't feel like it. We're 'married' remember?"

He winks, and I let out a laugh and tease, "I guess that means sex is off the table. You know… if we're married and all."

"We're in for an interesting stay, aren't we?" He says with a laugh. Shaking his head, he steps into me, heating up the already warm smile set on my lips. "Night, *babe.*"

"Sweet dreams, *honey.*"

He presses a kiss to my lips—one that is far too brief for my liking. For him too, I think, since he stays close even after pulling away, his eyes closed and his breathing picking up to an erratic and heady tempo. If he's trying to prove that this sort of relationship is more fun, he's failing miserably. I'm ready to screw the slow, medium temperature setting he's got on this thing and dial it up to the heat of a fresh relationship.

His hand leaves the back of my head and falls against his side. He shakes himself from his thoughts and puts on a grin before turning to the door.

"Night," he says again, and I chuckle at his drunken gait. When he starts down the hallway, I skip to the door to watch which room he'll be taking, but he starts heading toward the stairs.

"Hey!" I call out. His blue eyes lift up and catch mine over the very expensive-looking banister. "What room are you in?"

The corner of his mouth twitches, cratering his cheek. He nods to the door adjacent to mine, and then starts back down the stairs. I don't think I'm imagining the extra bounce in his step.

I duck back inside and shut the door, not only to keep my cats in, but to keep me from going out. I'm here for the amenities, for the view, for a staycation that I most definitely could use. I'm here to prove a point, and nothing more.

Nothing more.

I will not jump that man's bones; I will jump on that bed.

Using a running leap, I flop onto the mattress, scaring the hell out of my kitten and making the old, grumpy one hiss in my direction. I sink straight into the foam; this must be a Cozy King. It feels much like the fluffy bed used in the photo shoot. Perhaps I'm not so concerned about chasing down Cooper anymore; there is a major possibility I won't move from this spot my entire stay.

Tom hops onto my stomach, making me "oof" with the unexpected weight. He spins around and around and around, pawing at my t-shirt until he's finally satisfied with the spot and sprawls down. The purring calms the anxious pitter patter of my heart, like it always does. The magic cats carry are half the reason I own them. I plan to own many more.

My phone vibrates against my thigh, and being careful not to disturb Master Grumpy Butt, I wiggle it free from my jeans and hold it above my face.

Forgot to tell you... the Wi-Fi name is prettyflyforawifi. Password Monster2319.

I bite away at my smile and stroke Tom a few times so he's purring so loudly I can feel it in my stomach. He's got to calm these teenage butterflies. Seriously, I'm thirty now. I found another gray hair just the other day.

Couldn't just come in here and tell me? ;)

Honestly, I thought it would just look like an excuse to keep talking to you.

True

And it would be. It's my excuse now.

I laugh, rolling onto my stomach and knocking Tom onto the pillows with a snoozing Kat.

This is new for you, I type. *Usually you break the ice with something a normal person would keep to themselves.*

Like how I'm fighting the unbearable urge to put this conversation on hold and explore every inch of that intoxicating mouth of yours?

Oh sweet lord, is it hot in here? *Yes, like that for*

example.

Thought I'd try something else for a change.

Small talk?

No, he answers in a simple text before another follows. *Why don't you want to get married?*

This again?

For curiosity sake. I promise I won't ask again.

I contemplate my answer, starting my text and erasing it multiple times before I land on what the truth is. Because honestly, the deep rooted reason is a little embarrassing to admit. I spent the better half of my twenties guilty of one of the seven deadly sins in particular—envy. Julie and Jim had found their life partners so quickly it seemed. Holland was married before it was even legal to drink. Clearly on the outs having never gotten to that level of commitment, my thoughts went down wretched paths. When I wasn't insulting my own personality or body type, I thought horrible things about the people I loved most. As in, "if she can find someone, why can't I?" That sort of thing.

I hated it. I was a bitter, jealous girl who needed to stop and smell the roses. When I did, and found out all the things I had—work, sleeping in, an allowance to be selfish with my time, independence—I realized I wouldn't dare give *those* things up. And with everyone coming to me to vent about married people and parenting problems, I count myself very lucky.

I suppose when it didn't happen for me as quickly as it had for my siblings, I convinced myself that I never really wanted it in the first place.

It worked so well that you still don't want it, even if you have the chance for it in the future?

Yep. I bite away a grin and take a look out the balcony window next to the bed. The soft, transparent drapes bristle in the slight night wind. *Though I do admit, so far the fake married life isn't so bad. ;)*

Good. My evil plan is working. A pause, and then another message. *Any chance I've convinced you on actual marriage yet? ;)*

Persistence must be part of his advertising training. *I don't want the fiancé, kids, adult thing right now.*

Well, let me know if you ever do. Because I would fiancé you so hard.

I roll to my back again, laughing at the playfulness I can sense in his text tone. If the walls weren't so thick, I imagine I'd be able to hear him chuckling as well.

We spend the next ten minutes, thirty minutes, oh… it's been two hours chatting, minus the breaks when we both showered—in separate bathrooms—and when he got a call from his brother. I fluff the pillow and check the clock on the nightstand, telling myself *again* that I really should get to sleep, even though I can't imagine sleeping with my lady bits tingling like they are. Perhaps that shower should've been a cold one.

I should try to sleep now, I type, but it takes me a minute to actually send it.

Likewise. Though I doubt I'll resist the urge to keep talking to you.

A sleepy, goofy grin slides onto my lips. *Good luck with*

that. Goodnight. :)

Night, beautiful.

I stare at the texts, even scrolling through our conversation and reliving the evening again before I finally shake myself out of it and plug the phone in on the nightstand. Kat pounces up by my head, taking her usual spot on top of my hair to sleep. This is complete madness; all of it. The room itself as I let my sleepy eyes wander around it once more before I snuggle into the foreign pillows is enough to make me question my sanity. These things don't happen in real life, let alone to someone as insignificant as me. Successful, sexy, Pitt-in-his-prime kind of man, who is not just that, but also fun, unpredictable, and *adorable*, is my pretend husband while we play house in his billionaire buddy's home. Call the Hallmark channel; I have an idea for them.

I spin around in the sheets, causing Kat to give me an irritated look before she settles back down on a vacant pillow. With how late it is and the extreme comfort of this mattress, I'd have thought the moment I closed my eyes I'd drift off into wet dreams. Instead my fantasies are keeping me wide awake, and they are aching to be played out.

I clench my thighs together and try to sing an unsexy mantra in my head. The *Go Eat Worms* song I learned as a kid should work, but it doesn't. When I forget one simple lyric, my traitorous mind slides back into the memory of Cooper's lips on mine outside his truck just the other night. His beard was scruffier then, and I wonder how it will feel now that it's a bit more trimmed. That peck of a kiss he gave me earlier wasn't nearly long enough for me to tell.

"Gar," I grumble, twisting again in the sheets, burying my face ear-deep into the pillow. My fingers curl into the feathers as I try to suffocate the thoughts out of me. When I come closer to *actually* suffocating, I pull my face free and sit up on my knees. I blow a stray strand of hair from out of my eyes, sounding more horse than human. It's no use. If I'm going to get any sleep I'm going to have to alleviate some tension.

I look around the room, purely for instinctive reasons. It's been a while since I've done this. So long in fact, that poor B.O.B has a layer of dust on him. I haven't been this aroused since I saw a preview of Alexander Skarsgard in that very shirtless movie he starred in.

I let out a huff, grabbing at the hem of my tank top and pulling it over my head. Tom's sleepy growl vibrates the bed, reminding me that I'm not exactly alone. Not that my cats care if I play with myself, but I still can't get into the zone knowing that at any second a ball of fur could rub up against my leg.

Completely topless, I build a pillow fort around each of my cats, leaving me very little room—but enough room—to plop down on my back and run my hands over my bare stomach.

His hands are rougher, I think, disappointed that my too small and too soft hands can't convince me that he's the one who will be doing the touching. I'd also like to think that he wouldn't be frowning at the plushness of my stomach, the padding around my waistband, the stretch marks that we both know didn't come from a baby. I've always considered myself on the plus side, and if I'm being honest, I've contributed it to my single status. Telling myself that I don't want marriage anyway helps make that decision feel in my control.

Ugh, this is why I'm no good at pleasuring myself. I can't shut my damn mind off long enough to get there.

I let my fingers trail up to my breasts, taking a deep breath and letting it out. My mind cleanses all the insecure details and drifts off to Cooper and his heavenly blue eyes and the way his mouth moved when he called me gorgeous.

I circle a nail around a budding nipple, knowing that I can't quite imagine it as Cooper's finger, but I can imagine he's in the room watching. That he's at the foot of the bed, knuckles white as he clutches the bed frame, his boxer shorts strained and aching as I bring my other hand up to tease and pull the twin.

A hitch in my breathing makes me realize how loud I'm being. A rush of panic that he is *actually* hearing me pulls me right out of the fantasy, and not a moment too soon either, because at the buzz of my phone, a skittish kitten leaps onto my face.

"Kaff," I muffle through her fur, praising a deity that she didn't use her claws. I wriggle her off of me and roll over the pillow barrier I made. While grappling for my phone, I notice that I've been tossing, turning, and attempting to pleasure myself for nearly an hour.

Still trying to sleep, or is it just me?

A swoop in my stomach has me sitting back up on my

knees. I catch my reflection in the glass of the balcony doors, my face and topless half lit up by my phone. I can almost imagine Cooper knocking it out of my hands and pressing me into the mattress with the hard plate of his chest.

It is definitely not just you.

He doesn't reply back—well, it's only been ten, fifteen seconds—but I'm so ready to break some rules that I toss my phone on the bed and search around for my top. I pull it out from under my fat cat and slip it over my head on the way to the door.

I don't care if I said I get my own room. I don't care that sex was not on either of our agendas tonight. I need some damn sleep and some damn relief and it seems the only way I'm going to get it is—

"Oof!" I squeak at the same time I hear a low, baritone grunt. My body rocks back from the warm wall of muscle I've run smack into, and a hand reaches for my arm before I topple to my butt.

Cooper lets out a laugh, the warmth of his touch pebbling my breasts. I hide my face in his chest, laughing quietly with him, and only half realizing that there is no need to be quiet.

"Fancy meeting you here," he says through his laughter. His fingers brush through my hair and tilt my face up to his. There isn't a single moment of hesitation before he drops his lips to mine.

13

Sweet Relief

"I thought…" I say, my voice breathless and broken between our anxious lips. "I thought… sex… wasn't… on the table."

His lips turn up against mine, the hard plate of his chest pressing my back flat against the wall. "It's not," he breathes. "But we said nothing about the floor."

A lust-filled giggle slips out, the warm air around us zapping as his fingers trail down my neck. His palms cup my breasts as his tongue slides between my lips. My giddiness is suddenly silenced, replaced by the rush of heat in my lower abdomen. My knees buckle, my back arching into his touch. He's quickly erasing our surroundings, turning me into putty in his very capable hands.

There's a palm at my waist, tugging, pulling, fighting with the flimsy shirt I'm wearing. His touch is consuming all my thoughts; I'm only half aware of where my own hands are, though every flex of his hard muscle against my fingertips reminds me of the chiseled, cut man I'd been attempting to fantasize about in bed just moments earlier.

Another rush of warmth fills between my weakening legs. Am I even still standing? More like sunk into the carpet beneath our feet, and in the back of my mind I know this was against my self-imposed rules. I know it. I fight it, but then his fingers tuck into my waistband, and he gasps, "Five seconds." His lips are at my ear. "Five seconds is all the control I have." And because I only possess two seconds of control, I grasp his hand and curve his fingers into my neglected nethers before he can finish his countdown.

He's warm, almost unbearably so. The scruff along his face is scratching, tickling, taking me to a place I haven't been to in years. Oh yes, *years.* My nails scratch up his taut arm as his fingers tantalize and torture in the most pleasurable of ways. I pull at his hair, breathe into his open mouth and speak a language I've yet to master with him, yet we both seem rather fluent in it. His heavy-lidded eyes drift up to mine, and a smile teases at the corners of his mouth. He watches me come absolutely undone in his arms, a look close to that of someone winning the lottery etched into every line of his face. A rush of heat cascades down my entire being, from crown to pinky toe. I'm clawing at him, blinking stars out of my eyes, perspiring from the warmth of his breath on my neck. My mind is beyond comprehensible thought, and he says, "Hold onto me," and I somehow find the ability to comply, bringing my hand around his very impressive arousal.

His eyebrows rise, and a small laugh slips from between his panted breaths. "Not what... I meant..." he breathes, but doesn't stop me as I dive under the waistband of his boxers and reciprocate the favor he's so aptly giving me.

I'm losing it. My mind, my body, my everything. I feel myself rising to the peak of uncontrollable thoughts and actions, and my mouth connects with his shoulder, my teeth sink into the warm cotton of his shirt, and gone am I from this world.

"I'm sorry," I hear from somewhere outside of my body. "Damn it, I liked that one, too."

I shake my head, mind foggy as I fall back down into my feet. I'm tangled around Cooper, the hand I have wrapped around him moist with his release. I allow myself a small chuckle of amusement at being so far gone I hadn't noticed until now that he'd been out of this world with me.

He braces himself using the wall, caging me in. He shakes his head, his blond locks wet with exertion as if we'd been doing a more strenuous workout than just biceps and forearms.

"You weren't attached to it, were you?" he asks, dark blue eyes flicking to my shoulder. My brow furrows as I follow his gaze, then my mouth pops clean open at the sight of my tank top torn and hanging loosely off of my right breast.

"How dare you," I tease, prying my arm from the stickiness of our tight grasp and lifting the wardrobe casualty with my clean hand. The reminder that I wasn't too concerned about his clothing either has my gaze moving to his shoulder, and I bite back a grin as I nod to it. "I at least had the decency to rip on the seam."

An echoed confusion crosses his face as he plucks the

material off his skin and examines the teeny tiny hole I chewed in that very sexy white tee. I feel a giddy laugh erupt from his chiseled stomach still pressed with mine.

"Remind me to wear clothing every time this happens." His joking and post-pleasure eyes meet mine. "I'd rather you tear through this than skin."

"Likewise." The implication that this isn't just a one-time occurrence isn't lost on me, and a rush of heat slides down my neck, making me feel as if I need to lie down before I fall down.

Sensing the change in my spirits, he releases his hold on me, slowly pulling his arm back and taking a step toward the banister. The rush of cold air wakes me up enough to realize just how very naughty this was, and how even though it's a bad idea, I'd like to be that naughty with him again. And again. Maybe once more after that.

After tucking himself back inside his boxers, he reaches up to scratch the back of his head, and I admire the muscles in his arms and the talented tendons that run into his hands. I don't believe I've gotten off on a hand job alone unless it was just me. It could very well be attributed to the fact that it's been a very long time since Ms. O's been around, and Cooper is pretty much my blond-haired fantasy man.

"Think you can sleep now?" he asks with a lift of his lips. Even in the dark shadows of the hallway, I can see the dip in his cheeks from his laugh lines.

"After I wash off your man juice." I hold out my hand.

His laughter is bolting with genuine surprise and a bit of embarrassment. He closes the gap he put between us enough to kiss me sweetly on the lips. "Go out with me tomorrow?"

"Are you always going to ask me that question when my mind is otherwise occupied?"

"I'm three for three so far, so yes."

I push back on his chest. "I'd like to stay in," I say, careful not to say yes, but not to say no either.

"Done." He kisses me once more, letting this one linger. "Sleep well… you know, after you get my 'man juice' off of ya."

I wipe my hand on the butt of his boxers with an evil glint in my eye. I shrug at his mock shocked expression. "What? You're washing them anyway, right?"

He shakes his head at me, boldly hooking his thumbs into the waistband and pulling his boxers to the floor. He stoically marches to his room, completely bottomless. My joke is rewarded with a great view of his perfect ass that will most likely star in my dreams tonight, if I manage to get any sleep at all.

***

A low rumbling sound rouses me from a vivid, yummy dream, and I blink myself into the present, heart thumping hard under a borrowed t-shirt. Tom picks up his head as I sit up, stretching his arms out as he too wakes up to the sound of a motor streaming in through my open balcony doors.

Once my heart has calmed and my mind has woken up, I wipe away the sweat from my silly sleepy behavior and scoot from under the fluffy comforter. Kat jerks when I step out onto the balcony, eying me before turning back toward the birds in the very leafy tree that stands next to the house. I cover a yawn, lean on the railing, and gaze out at the unconventional alarm clock.

Cooper's blond head comes into focus across the very large backyard, bouncing as he tries to turn the riding lawn mower around. A sleepy laugh flits from my lips when he gets out of one position only to get stuck in another. Judging by his body language, I imagine some mighty cursing is happening under the sound of the mower.

Tom runs his spine against my ankle, and I nod. "I know, right? You'd think this place had a gardener or twenty."

I shrug and head back inside, glancing at the clock on the nightstand before flicking the alarm off. Not bothering to close the windows since I'm three stories up and the nearest neighbor is about fifty acres away, I strip down and head into that luxurious shower, really taking the time to enjoy it. Last night I was more preoccupied with Cooper's text messages than the four stream jet shower. Now… that showerhead sure looks like it wants to get to know me on an intimate level, but maybe I'll save that until it's seen me naked at least three times.

Knowing my anal tendencies about punctuality, I regretfully turn the hot, relaxing shower off about twenty minutes in, wrap myself up in a fluffy blue towel, and step into the massive bedroom that—if I'm not careful—would convince me into marrying Cooper on the spot just to own one of these. The sound of the mower still carries into my room, louder now, and when I peek outside I find Cooper a stone's throw away from the house. Looks like he's finally gotten the hang of that thing.

I wolf whistle, not sure if he'll even hear me, but his head crooks up, and with his eyes locked on my very sexy towel-on-the-head look, he runs the mower straight into the fence around the basketball court. Even with all the noise from the mower, I catch the curse he drops that time.

Laughing—and a little flushed from the unexpected reaction—I turn back inside and get dressed in my realtor best. There are a few showings I have set up for today, one of my buyers is signing on his new house, and I promised Sarah a lunch to divulge all my dirty secrets of the biz as she moves from promising intern to passing her test. While all of that was enough to make me anxious to get to work a week ago, I'm now anxious to get there only to come back here and see what Cooper cooks up for me for our stay-in date tonight. I could go for a nice cuddle on the couch while binge-watching Netflix, with a side of orgasm, please. For all his ridiculous notions, I will give him that skipping the hoops a person has to jump through just to get to the sex is a very good idea. He wants "marriage?" Watch out, buddy, I will give you marriage. I don't even plan on turning on any beauty tools when I get back from work.

I slip on my Michael Kors heels, reminding myself that I'll need to paint my toenails soon since we're in sandal weather and I can't wait to put those suckers on. Then again, if I'm not going to worry about making myself super adorable twenty-four seven, then perhaps I won't.

"I'll see you guys tonight," I tell my kitties. "Behave,

you got me? No pissing on any of those sheets just because you don't think they're yours yet." Yeah, dogs aren't the only ones to do that. I narrow my eyes at Tom, his lazy green eyes gazing back as if saying he'll do whatever he wants whenever he wants. I point a finger to emphasize my point. "I'm talking to you, Professor Grumpy Pants."

I continue "the look" until I've shut them in, hoping that they'll use the litter box I put on the balcony and not the $300 loafers in the closet.

Skipping right past the kitchen, I head outside, keys in hand, ready to make a stop at Buy a Bagel for breakfast. Cooper turns around the corner, wiping the sweat from the nape of his neck with a towel. His lips curl up into that knee-melting smile, and he nods to my wittle VW.

"You heading out?"

"Ain't no rest for the wicked."

He closes the distance between us rather quickly for a man who looks like he's just run a marathon. Pressing a soft palm at the small of my back, he pulls me in enough for a light peck on the lips that while it's so simple, it steals my breath away. I refuse to believe that sensation continues after a couple has been together past the initial spark, though the thought does come into my mind that maybe there is something to be said about simplicity.

My head tilts as he pulls away, and I let my curious gaze float up to his. "Can I ask you something?"

His eyebrow twitches up. "Yeah."

"Why are you mowing the lawn?"

His expression relaxes as he runs a hand over his

growing beard. "I like doing things myself first. No sense in paying someone to do something I can do."

"Hmm."

"Hmm," he mocks my non-response. I roll my eyes and put a teasing hand into his very hard stomach.

"Bye." And just to show that I'm taking my role as fake wife seriously, I push up on my toes and give him another simple peck. See how he does with a not-enough kiss.

Satisfied with the surprise in his eyes, I slide my sunglasses down and take my spot behind the wheel. Thank heavens I've got a busy schedule to distract me from how long it'll be until I can tease him again.

14

Crowns and Frowns

I open the door to the huge mansion, anticipation of seeing Cooper again after a very long day making my hands a little shaky on the knob. My tummy tickles are somewhat quieted when I walk into a giant smoke cloud.

"Cooper?" I ask, coughing through the fog. I duck down below the smoke line, squinting toward the kitchen, expecting to see giant yellow and red flames.

"It's all good!" he calls back. "I'm cool, I got this."

The high-pitched chirp of the smoke detectors start going off, and I slap my hands over my ears as I wade through the thick cloud. Cooper is jumping up to press the alarm off, dishtowel thrown over his shoulder and a questionable stain on his blue button-down.

I rush over to open a window, then quickly unlock the back patio doors and spread them wide. Cooper takes the towel draped over his shoulder and starts using it to direct the smoke outside. As it dissipates, I catch the open oven and a full stove top—the sources of the unfortunate air around us.

"Didn't want to hire a chef either, huh?"

His nose wrinkles. "I don't suppose you'd like to help me out?"

A smile creeps onto my lips, and I slither past him to see what the damage is. "What were you trying to make?" I ask, lifting a brow at the blackened indiscernible food.

"Chicken Parmesan." He runs a hand through his blond locks. "Apparently it was a little too advanced for this bachelor."

"Oh, but you aren't a bachelor right now." I give him a pointed look as I test several different drawers before finding an apron. His eyes watch me with careful concentration as I tie it around my waist. I'm extremely thankful that it fits. How embarrassing would that be if I couldn't get the sucker into a bow while attempting to look all domestic?

I stand up straight, settling my hands on my hips. In the back of my mind I thought that rocking the "mom" look my sister usually dons would give him a hard dose of reality—this isn't flattering on anyone, let alone someone who just got home from an achingly long day at work. However, judging by the dazed expression that has settled on his face, you'd think I'd taken clothing off, not put more on.

My mouth pools so suddenly that I have to gulp, and I struggle to maintain the teasing tone I've grown accustomed to in his presence. "Do you have any more chicken?"

He blinks himself free from his thoughts, grinning as if he didn't just imagine me in some kinky housewife-type fantasy. "Don't think it's salvageable, huh?"

"I'm not eating it." I laugh, poking at the burnt mess

135

with a fork.

"Damn." His shoulders slump next. "I used it all."

His body is so close that the heat from the leftover smoke isn't the only heat that's causing my skin to flush. Taking a step back to keep my wits about me, I lean against the kitchen island and tap my nails near the cutting board.

"What else you got?"

He shrugs, slapping the dishtowel against the island by my hip. "Whey protein." His shoulders shake as he laughs at my grimace. "Feel like take-out?"

A sigh of relief deflates my entire body. "Please." I tear the apron off, slapping it onto the island watching as disappointment fills his expression as I strip myself from the domestic item.

In a moment of complete curiosity, I unbutton the top button of my pencil skirt and let my tummy loose— something I normally do the second I get home from work, but I've held that in for the sake of saving present company from seeing me so Homer Simpson.

Cooper confirms my theory, his lips turning up at the sight of me completely letting go, a rush of heat rising behind those blue irises. I'm so not used to these kinds of reactions to such simple, very human-like things. I wonder if I burped if he'd whisk me away for a night of torrid lovemaking.

His eyes lift to meet mine. "Also… I do have a chef. I'm reminded of why."

I chuckle, nodding at his very accurate assessment of his cooking skills. Not that I can talk. Chicken Parm would be a little too advanced for me as well.

"I'm gonna get out of these," I tell him, gesturing to my realtor wardrobe. On my way up the staircase, I make my dinner requests over my shoulder. "I like Hawaiian pizza and stuffed cheesy bread. Or if you go the Chinese route, I like mandarin chicken and beef and broccoli."

"You sure you don't need help getting out of those?" he calls up after me. I answer by tossing my jacket clean over his adorable face. I have a few theories I want to test tonight, and that smile will weaken my resolve to keep my distance long enough to prove their validity.

***

Any given weekday night, I'd have my feet kicked up on the coffee table, an overlarge, holey shirt draped over my braless bosom, and boxer shorts. Tom and Kat would join me as I flicked through my streaming options and gorged on a party size bag of peanut butter M&Ms. This night, however, is far from the norm.

I know I'm supposed to be playing wifey. Not just any wifey, but a longtime wifey. My single life attire would be appropriate in that relationship, because by then the two individuals have seen more than they've bargained for, and seeing that would be expected. Maybe anticipated.

It's why I'm not donning the "vegging" look tonight. Because I believe Mr. Family Man is turned on more by that version of me than the one I actually put an effort into. Thinking back to that first kiss, no wonder he couldn't keep his hands to himself. I was the living embodiment of frumpy.

I'm not dissing that look in the slightest, or anyone who

is attracted to such a thing, I just honestly haven't met a soul who is, or at least stayed with them long enough to find out. So I pulled out all the stops tonight just to see if he'd find a tight dress, makeup, dolled up curls, and stilettos as attractive as pajamas.

Smoothing my dress down my body, I nibble at my lip and start having second thoughts about the form-fitting attire. I've gotten compliments on it before, many times actually. Witnessed blind dates dropping their jaw and then grinning like an idiot the rest of the evening. I even dubbed it my "get lucky" dress at one point, but in the well-lit master bathroom, I start to doubt my sex appeal, especially if I don't get as epic of a reaction from Cooper as I do from slipping an apron on.

"I look okay, right?" I ask Kat who's perched on the counter, pawing at one of my hair ties. Since she's not the best girl to get an honest opinion from, I grab my phone, snap a bathroom pic, and then send it to Holland.

Hawt!

I clack back, Promise??

You have no idea how jealous I am, she writes. I miss lucky dresses.

I send her a thank you along with a reassurance that she looks adorable with her baby belly and fight the temptation to tell her to stop complaining since I doubt she'll ever find herself buying the same pants size as me, maternity section and all. But as she often reminds me, I got the dream boobs so *I'm* the one who can't complain. The grass really is always greener... but just wait until her pregnancy chest comes in.

Then she really will have it all.

Feeling not exactly confident, but confident enough with my choice of wardrobe, I connect my phone to the charger and let my heels sink into the soft carpet as I cross the room. A wave of nervous energy buzzes up and down my spine, causing a warm flush to settle in my cheeks. I imagine this is how girls felt when they walked down the staircase before prom, their dream date waiting at the bottom and their parents at the ready with a camera, and all they can think is, dear god, I hope I don't fall on my face.

I never went to my prom. Just another one of those things I hoped for that never happened.

The smoke has left the building, now only the soft light of the setting sun filling up the very open concept house. I suck in a breath, not only to hold in my stomach, but so I can concentrate fully on not tumbling face over foot down that intimidating staircase.

I make it to the main landing with zero damages. Glancing around for my "husband," I let out a laugh at how silly I feel after my anti-climactic entrance.

"Hello?" I call out, wondering if he also went upstairs to change out of his smoke-filled clothing. Even if he had, I doubt he'd take as long as I did to get ready.

"Um… I hate to do this…" his low voice says from the back guest bathroom. Amused and confused, I clack my way over to him.

"Hate to do what?"

He pokes his head out, the bottom half of his face covered with his hand. But his eyes do give me an appreciative once over that, if I wasn't concerned about what's going on, I'd take the time to compare it to his earlier reaction.

I raise an eyebrow, and he slowly takes his hand from his mouth, opening wide to show me a very noticeable hole where a back tooth should be sitting.

I jerk backward. "What the…"

"I think I need a dentist."

A small laugh escapes me. "I'd say so." I step up to him, touching his face gently to examine the damage. His breath smells fresh and minty, the scent only somewhat distracting me. "Does it hurt?"

He nods, making a grunting sound of assent through his wide open mouth. "Pwetty sure itsa cwown."

"What was that?"

He relaxes his jaw. "Think I lost a crown while flossing."

"Nice to know you floss."

He attempts a face at me, but is distracted by what I assume is a ping of pain over the exposed nerve. His hand shoots up to grab his jaw, and his eyes pinch close for a brief moment.

Having left my phone upstairs, I boldly pat the front pocket of his jeans. He jerks in surprise, but relaxes when he realizes I'm only grabbing his cell. Though, I do run a thumb up a growing muscle accidentally-on-purpose on my journey to extract the phone.

"Do you have a dentist's number?"

He snorts at me like that's a ludicrous question. I pull

140

out Google, ask him who he has for insurance, and he babbles answers off at me without a shred of hesitation. Full name, social security number, date of birth, dental hygiene history. Having him so willing to share that information has my curiosity reeling, and my lips turn into a wicked grin in the glow of the screen light.

"Sexually active?" I ask, even if it's not part of the questionnaire. He catches on quick, leaning against the bathroom doorframe, his minty breath washing over me.

"Not currently, but definitely in the near future."

I playfully roll my eyes up to him, but there is a rush of heat that rests just below my belly. I press my thighs together and remind myself that he is in too much pain to make "near future" into the present.

"Okay, I got you in with a Dr. Jenkins at a clinic by my office. They do late emergency work." I slip his phone into the top of my dress and flick my gaze up to his. Even while clutching at his jaw, his tongue pressing against the inside of his cheek, the look he gives me is so stomach-joltingly gorgeous I lose my train of thought momentarily. He lifts his free hand up, stroking a single finger across my forehead, brushing away a curl.

A hot shiver runs up my spine, setting off goosebumps up and down my arms. The corner of his lip lifts before there is a slight wince of pain in his expression.

"Thank you," he says, almost reverently, his voice low and dripping like honey. I feel it in the depths of my chest, shocking my heart into a frenzied rhythm. I have to swallow hard and blink my gaze away from his to get a grip on myself.

Smiling my way out of the daze, I playfully tap the back of my hand against his stomach. "Let's go."

He follows me outside, grabbing his wallet and keys while still holding his jaw. I've never been a nurturing sort, but I like the idea of taking care of a strong wall of muscle who has been taken down by something as human as a toothache. I don't blame him; those suckers hurt like a bitch. I've had one root canal in my lifetime, and I don't revel in the idea of experiencing it a second time.

Saving him from having to squish into my bug, I hold my hands out for the keys to his truck. His bushy eyebrow lifts, and after a reluctant pause in which we have a quiet stand-off, he relinquishes the right to sit behind the wheel of the Mud Monster. I don't exactly blame him for that either—he has driven with me before. I put Cruella De Vil to shame in terms of aggressive driving, but since he's putting so much faith in me, I decide that I'm going to be especially careful with his six-figure investment on wheels.

Cooper gets called back almost immediately after we arrive, the office dead now that it's after hours. The receptionist offers him an ice pack, and I internally chastise myself for not thinking of that earlier. I chalk it up to the fact that I'm completely out of my element. Have to say, I've never gotten to the point in a relationship where I make appointments and escort my SO on errands. If this was part of his plan to show me that sparks will fly even during the mundane, talk about commitment.

"Don't let me take Loritab," he tells me, sliding in to

the dentist reclining seat. "It will be your top most regret."

I set my hand on the headrest, running my thumb nail over his blond locks. "It sounds like it will provide memorable entertainment."

His eyes roll back at my touch, heavy lids closing as I run my fingers through his hair. An amused grin teases the corner of my mouth as he lifts a finger to press it to his lips. "Shh," he says. "You've found my off button."

Warmth starts to spread from my fingertips to my thumping heart. Giving him innocent pleasure fascinates and confuses me in equal measure, and a stray thought flies across my mind, a thought I've never had before—I could very well have a lifetime of just this and find myself happier than I've ever been.

My fingers pause, tangled in the soft strands of blond and silver. I shake my head hard, closing my eyes even to banish the thought back to where it originated from. Cooper shifts under my hand, and I pull away, opening my eyes and forcing a grin. I'm saved from having to answer the concern in Cooper's pulled eyebrows when the dentist walks in.

"Well," he says, eyes skating over my dress before flicking to Cooper in sympathy. "I bet this isn't how you expected the night to go."

Cooper chuckles, meeting my gaze briefly before answering Dr. Jenkins. "I did have other plans for my mouth."

An embarrassed—and I admit, flattered—flush rises up my neck, and I playfully backhand him in the shoulder.

"That mouth's gonna get you in trouble."

The dentist chuckles at our banter, settling in to the swivel chair next to Cooper. He slides on a glove and coaxes Cooper's chin down. "Let's take a look, shall we?"

Cooper opens his mouth so wide that I'm fairly impressed by it, but it's not surprising. With how often he lets it run, I'd be more surprised if he had a small mouth.

"Yep, definitely lost that crown." He pulls his finger from Cooper's chompers and leans back in his seat to address the both of us. I thought I'd feel uncomfortable, maybe even overstepping my boundaries by being here. Yet, it feels as natural as breathing. That thought is the only thing that makes me shift slightly toward the door.

"I can put in a temp for now. Cover that nerve while you two continue your evening. Then we can put in a permanent replacement tomorrow afternoon."

Cooper shakes his head. "We have plans we can't break."

My brow furrows, and a speck of amusement dusts his blue irises.

"Babysitting, Maya."

"Right." I laugh, shaking my head at myself. It's funny how he remembers agreeing to watch *my* niece and nephew more than I do.

"Next opening I have is on Monday," Dr. Jenkins says. "The temp should last the weekend."

"Sounds good."

"I'll write you a prescription for—"

"Ibuprofen," I interject. "Apparently, this guy can't take anything stronger than that."

He chuckles at Cooper nodding like a bobble-head. "All right, then. Let's get that temp in there. You'll be back to your date in twenty minutes, tops. Wouldn't want to waste that spectacular dress on a night here."

I smile in appreciation, warmth touching my cheeks as the dentist scopes out my "lucky" attire once more. Cooper lifts an eyebrow up at me. Those blue eyes, while showing how much pain he truly is in, also have a hint of admiration swirling in them.

"No offense, Doc. But I don't think it's the dress."

15

Cruel Birth Control

"H-holy cow," Katie says through her wide open mouth. I chalk exhaustion up to the lack of filter. If the mansion wasn't enough of a shock, the second her eyes land on my housemate she seems to lose coherent thought. She nearly drops the car seat hooked on her arm, and Cooper is quick to relieve her of it.

"Nice to meet you," he says, then turns that fun-loving, adorable grin to the almost two-month-old in the car seat. "And you too, little man."

Katie chokes on what could only be air, and I'm sure Jim would call her out on the gawking if he wasn't doing the same thing to the TV.

I bite back a laugh at their reactions, wondering if that is exactly how I looked when I first saw Cooper… and the TV, for that matter.

Claire seems to be the only one capable of saying anything, and with one hand clinging to Jim and the other pointing straight up at Cooper, she says, "Kitty!"

Cooper's brows bunch, and he whips around. "Where?" I stifle my laughter, a snort rumbling my nose at his overreaction. He still hasn't gotten used to Tom and Kat and has done his best to avoid them entirely. That's going to change at some point during this experiment, I'm sure of it.

Katie lets out a shaky laugh that seems to takes her out of her daze. "Sorry. She's not used to seeing facial hair."

Jim tears his eyes from the TV to give his wife a look. My brother has been a giant supporter of the fresh face, mostly for the hygienic aspect. He's a bit OCD, and any sprout of fuzz along his chin causes his mind to get extremely itchy.

Cooper grins, crouching down to settle the car seat on the floor and get eye level with my niece. "You like kitties?"

"No!"

He faux gasps, then sticks his bottom lip out in a playful pout. I really do wish him luck; that girl will not be warming up to anyone anytime soon.

Claire sticks her tongue out and blows a wet raspberry, then scurries past us to destroy whatever room she finds first, singing a song in a language that I swear isn't English.

"Claire Liza Baker!" Katie sighs, dropping the diaper bag to the ground. "I'm so sorry," she apologizes to Cooper. I raise an eyebrow because she's never apologized for Claire's behavior around me, but perhaps that's because I'm family.

Cooper waves her off, straightening from his crouch. "That's pretty polite for a two-year-old from what I've heard."

A crash sounds from the back hallway, and my brother

rushes off to see what sort of trouble Claire's causing. I reach for the good child before I get stuck dealing with the other one. Cooper wants kids? Claire may convince him otherwise, and I'll prove my point without uttering a single word.

"There should be enough milk in there for the day," Katie says as I unbuckle the sweet, *quiet*, little boy. I may not want babies, but they have the *best* smell. I cradle his tiny body to my chest, inhaling the fresh scent of baby shampoo off his soft head. He's so warm and squishy, if they didn't grow into that chaos creator back there, then I'd be all for making babies.

"He's getting a rash under his little balls. So make sure you get the cream on there." She starts digging around in her bag. "I think I packed the powder... it's in here somewhere I think. If not, that's fine. But use the cream. Poor guy hasn't been sleeping well because of it. Oh! And he is a projectile burper. I'd cover up with more than just a rag after he's done eating."

Got it... make Cooper burp the baby.

Katie clutches her head, muttering to herself, "What else...?"

"Relax," I tell her. "It's not like I haven't done this before."

She laughs, her mouth tired and her eyes at half-mast. I hope my brother treats her to a much needed nap before a much needed romp. But judging by the anxious look in his eyes when he comes back down the hall with Claire on his hip, I highly doubt a nap is anywhere in his mind.

"There are snacks for that one"—Katie nods to her

"Aya, Aya," Claire says, pulling on my pant leg, proudly holding up her diaper. "I pee pee."

I hang my head and let out a long sigh. Of course, *that* I understand.

***

My eyes drift up to the massive, decorative clock hanging on the wall in the living room, half the toys from the kid's room burying me from the waist down as I sip on fake tea—that I'm pretending is wine—with my niece. It's only been an hour since I passed off the crying baby, and only three since Jim and Katie left to have a day of... not this. How in the world do they do it every day?

"Moobak tafolrof sitvia," Claire babbles, smacking the teapot against the eyeball of a stuffed horse.

"Uh huh." My go-to response for this "tea party." I don't want to poke the bear; the one time I said, "What, sweetie?" she threw herself flat on her back and screamed at the ceiling.

She yawns, her small mouth opening wide as she relaxes into the horde of stuffed animals. I slowly, cautiously, pluck myself free from all the dress up clothes, play sets, and baby dolls, hoping another screaming session isn't pending when I get to my feet.

Claire hardly seems to notice my movement, her eyelids drooping. The teapot slips from her fingers as she drifts off.

I have maybe twenty minutes if I'm lucky. With the house suddenly so quiet, I tiptoe over all the toys and head out back to Cooper, holding my breath and hoping Chase too has drifted off to sleep.

Cooper turns his head at the sound of the sliding glass door. He gives me a half-smile, one that is a little lackluster from his usual grin.

"Hey," I mouth.

"Hey," he whispers back. Chase sniffles in his sleep against Cooper's shoulder. "It's awfully quiet in there."

"Out here, too." I take a seat next to him in the twin chaise lounge. "You want to make a break for it?"

He chuckles. "Hell no. This is the part that makes it all worth it."

My brow raises, like, *uh-huh, sure.* He only grins at my skepticism.

"I love it," he says, adjusting in the chair, careful not to disturb the baby against his shoulder. "The noise, the chaos, then the quiet moments that make you wonder what you did to deserve such little blessings."

"I don't think you're using that word right."

"I'd have fifty of them, if I could."

I fight away a yawn. "How many do you really want?"

He presses his lips together in thought, his hand patting the tiny bundle in his arms. I have to say, while I scoff at the fake family of the Hallmark card, I feel as if I could snap a picture right now, send it into their headquarters, and make millions.

"Four," he says after a minute. "Maybe six."

"*Six?*"

"Gotta be an even number." He adjusts again, and I wonder if his rear is past the point of numb.

"Why not two?" I point out while secretly wondering if

154

zero is an even number.

He shakes his head. "I want more than two."

I rest my chin in my hand, completely puzzled by this man. You'd think after today two would be too many.

"So why an even number?"

"Buddy system," he says without hesitation. "Disneyland, Universal Studios, water parks, flights… everyone's gotta have a partner." He leans in with a wink. "No child left behind."

I suck in a breath, warming from head to toe from his proximity. His skin is sun-kissed and gorgeous, and I let out a frustrated sigh at his beauty. It's not fair; why can't a man this breathtaking be interested in a fling?

"Even spouting crazy talk, you are very sexy, Mr. Sterling."

He laughs. "Likewise, Ms. Baker."

I have the urge to plant a kiss on his lips, but I'm interrupted halfway on my quest to close the distance by a crash coming from inside, followed by an "Uhhhhh ohhhhhh."

Cooper lets out a laugh at my pouty frown, and before I can even move, he offers me the sleeping child instead. And I gladly accept.

***

Cooper and I wave at a rejuvenated Jim and Katie as they take their children far far away from here. The second Cooper closes the door, we both fall back against it and slide to the floor. If I agree to babysit for ten hours again, someone please check me for early signs of senility.

I roll my head toward Cooper at the same time he rolls his to me, and I let out a laugh and run a finger over that red mark still on his cheek. His smile forms, denting a dimple under my nail.

"That was fun," he says, and he actually means it.

"Strange, strange man," I muse, shaking my head against the door. The house is a disaster. Toys strewn every which way, uncapped markers on a high shelf in an attempt to keep them from a two-year-old magician... who managed to undress herself five times throughout the day and made sharp and dangerous objects appear in her little hands. There's a strong smell of spit-up hanging in the air, mixed with yet another burnt meal... my fault this time. After starting a pot of noodles, a poopy scent reached my nostrils and even the most advanced of diaper changers would have spent twenty minutes on that mess.

The moment Katie and Jim rang the doorbell, relief covered every inch of me. I gratefully handed over the half-naked children and rushed them out the door. Though, it was nice to get a squishy hug from Claire before she left. I wasn't too fond of the very wet and chocolately kiss she left on my jeans. On closer inspection, I doubt even the toughest detergent is gonna get that out.

Cooper leans over, and before I realize what he's doing, his lips are on mine in a gentle, soft kiss.

"Thank you."

"Huh?" I say, swaying a little from the unexpected display of affection.

"For giving me a day with kids." He blinks a set of tired

156

eyes, a light smile on his lips. "There aren't that many in my life."

I chuckle through a yawn. "No wonder you like them. I'm surrounded by the little runts."

He only gives me a tired, curious glance. I let out a breath and feel myself slipping into a sleepy babble.

"Well, my brother has those two," I say, lazily tapping against the door. "My sister and her husband have four. My partner at work has three. And my best friend has one on the way."

"Wow," he says, and I'm grateful he appreciates that it really is a lot of children. "What's the age range?"

"The oldest is Lucas… he's ten. And Chase is the youngest at 2 months, unless you count Holland's bun."

"Holland's your best friend?"

I nod, covering yet another yawn. My limbs are starting to turn to jelly. "She's coming up on her tenth anniversary. She and her husband always wanted to wait to have kids, so they're just starting now."

He lets out a low hum, letting me know he's still listening, but I think we're both starting to drift. Going from one extreme to another is tiring, and it's catching up to me.

"When did you decide you didn't want them?"

I have to lift my eyelids, not realizing that I'd closed them. "Not everyone wants kids, Cooper."

"I know," he says. "I don't mean to offend. It's only… you mentioned that when things didn't happen for you, you'd convinced yourself you never wanted them. I'm curious about when that was."

157

My mind is way too done to think about the answer. And even if I was one hundred percent alert, I'm not sure if there is one. "I don't know," I say. "My brother's wedding, maybe." I pause, second guessing myself. "Maybe before that."

His lazy smile twitches, eyes scanning over my face and then down my arm before he tangles his fingers with mine.

"May I sleep with you?"

I frown. "As delicious as that sounds, I really don't think I have the energy to—"

"I mean actual sleep." He taps his forehead to mine. "I can see you're dozing off, and I am too. But I'm not quite ready to say goodnight."

My lips turn up, and I nod as enthusiastically as I can muster. Though I don't think I've made a case for my life logic at all today, and I really should, I'm not ready to admit that actually sleeping together sounds so much better right now than "sleeping" together.

16

We All Fall

Given the fact that I went to bed utterly exhausted, I'm not surprised that I wake up to a glorious Sunday morning… that is technically almost afternoon.

Shifting in the soft and fluffy sheets, I breathe in a satisfied breath of fresh air, the balcony doors left open once again so my cats can find their way to their litter box in the middle of the night. My body feels as if I've slept on a bed of clouds, a little sore from the constant up and down from the floor to chasing a toddler, but for the most part, very much content.

Cooper and I spent most of last night lazily conversing until we fell asleep. I don't even remember if I finished the sentence I was saying, but he obviously didn't notice or didn't care because I didn't wake up once after I drifted off.

It was nice, though. I try to think back to a moment when I fell asleep next to someone I hadn't already stripped naked with. There were a few, but they didn't last long. After the initial infatuation, there was nothing left but sex. When that too lost its appeal, they moved on or I did. I don't remember a time when cuddling was something to look forward to or even enjoy. It felt too serious. Yet, last night was... not perfect, but whatever word comes closest to it.

I roll my head to look at my bedmate who is still sound asleep. He is a radiator; the heat pouring off of him hot enough to melt a candle in under a minute. I don't mind it at the moment. Even with the summer air floating inside the cool house, I snuggle up to him, tucking my head in the warmth of his chest.

That heat rushes straight between my legs, the simple act of pressing against him giving me a not so subtle reminder that it's been a while since I've been in bed with a man. And a loooong while since I've been in bed with a man I was so attracted to that I'd fake a marriage with him just to spend some more time together.

I squeeze his middle, and he stirs in my arms. A sleepy smile spreads across his lips, and he plops a heavy arm on my waist. A low grumble vibrates through my cheek as he groans into my hair, and another wave of fire fills my lower abdomen when he thrusts his hips against me.

Ah... one of the perks of waking up next to a man. Spooning is a very different—and usually unwanted— surprise, but waking up forking? Well, let's just say I prefer cake to ice cream.

I really appreciate what sleep does to a man, and with my body on the search for relieving the tension that's been building at a much faster rate since I met him, I press down on him and rock my hips playfully, holding back a moan from the surge of pleasure that sparks across every inch of my skin.

His grin widens. "Please tell me I'm awake."

I tilt my lips up toward his, seeking them out with soft, yet urgent kisses. As soon as I get a hold of his mouth, his hand cups my cheek, holding me in place as his tongue slides across mine in one smooth, sensual movement.

I'm losing my head already. While every kiss he's delivered has been an electric shock straight to my core, this one is almost orgasm-worthy. I rock my hips even harder into him, hoping to get some much-needed relief.

He chuckles into my mouth, leaning up on an arm to hover over me. His hand goes back to my face, holding me as if I'm something to be savored. It's a unique feeling to be on the receiving end of something that seems so loving and caring. In all my naughty escapades, I've never come across a man who treats a woman he's only known for a short while as a longtime lover. In the back of my mind, I wonder if he's only kissing and touching me in this way because this is how he believes married couples express intimacy, or if it is truly how he is in bed.

I wriggle underneath him, ready to speed things up before my mind becomes too laden with thoughts that will take me out of the moment. My fingers start to tug and pull at his hair, his clothing, my hips rocking upward now in an attempt to get him to go faster. Cooper chuckles at my enthusiasm, taking my anxious hands and moving them up over my head.

"In a hurry?" he asks, the blue in his eyes bright with

the sunlight streaming through the balcony.

"Mmm-hmm," I say with gusto, pushing out my bosom to emphasize my point. The dimple in his cheek makes its first appearance of the day, and it's so adorable that I feel my heart leap from my chest momentarily.

A flash of amusement crosses his expression, and then he flattens himself on top of me, my body molding to his like we're two pieces from different puzzles that surprisingly fit one another. He strokes my wild bed hair away from my face, gazing at me with a playful smile set on his kissed lips.

"You, my dear, are a bed hog."

I wrinkle my nose at him. "Well, you *dearie*, need a breathe-right strip."

"We ran the ad for the last campaign of those." He juts a finger over his shoulder. "I gave a bunch of samples to my buddy, actually."

"Do they work?"

He shrugs. "Don't know. Maybe we can test one out on *you* tonight. I wasn't the only one sawing logs."

I playfully smack his shoulder, our laughter moving against each other in ways that has us both swapping our smiles for gasps of pleasure.

My hips attempt another roll up against him, and he hangs his head, the blond ends of his hair tickling the bridge of my nose.

"Maya? I'm… I'm falling for you," he blurts out in frustration. My heart goes from passionate throbbing to thick, heavy thumping. His eyes turn apologetic, as if he knows just how fragile I am about the particular subject. "I know I joked about it when you agreed to come here, but I in no way thought it would happen this fast."

"Really?" I say, hoping my voice stays light and flirtatious. "Given what I already know of you, I think this confession is actually coming a little late."

A rare rush of pink tints his cheeks, and he groans, burying his face into the pillow by my head. The weight of his body should be killing me, but it actually feels so good that I'm having a hard time finding enough brain cells to talk to him about this. Most of them are working overtime in the hypothalamus department.

"I'm sorry," he muffles into the feathers, and I nudge him back up to look him in the eye. If I'm being honest with myself, he's the closest anyone's ever come to being part of any future I could imagine. The fact still remains though that I don't want children. I don't want a settled life. This game we're playing is far more dangerous than I thought, and the smart part of me knows that I should wriggle myself free. I should pack my bags, take my cats back home, and find Cooper a place to live so that we can both move on from this nonsense experiment. My mind and heart knows it's the right thing to do, but my body aches with the thought. My body wants so much to be right here, underneath him, feeling his taut muscles against my soft curves. It's so unfair to have this conversation in bed, because my heart and mind just have no chance of winning.

"Please," I whisper. "Don't fall for me."

His eyes search mine, and while I can sense his disappointment I can also see the flirtatious side of him, that hungry male who has a ready and willing female at his disposal.

"It's not fair to have this conversation with you underneath me."

We finally have a shared thought. "You started it."

He brings his lips down on mine, cupping my face again to hold me in place. The kiss is more urgent, more frantic than his slow build, and I drown in it, let it erase our dialogue, erase my guilt and allow me to focus on only the sensations he causes under my skin.

His thumb strokes down the side of my face, making me shiver with anticipation. It's so incredibly titillating to have such a simple caress cause such havoc in my body. My nipples harden under the weight of his chest, and the small amount of uncovered skin on my stomach burns against his abdominals. I feel as if there is another version of me trying to claw her way out. I roll my hips, faster and faster, getting closer to my eminent release.

"Maya," Cooper grunts between our lips, distracting me for a moment. "Not that I want you to stop, but... could you please move your cat?"

Shocking me out of the moment, I lift my head to find Kat rubbing up against Cooper's leg. A giggle slips from my lips, shaking my stomach against his heated skin.

"Of all the times to cuddle," I mutter, pushing the ball of my foot into the kitten's fur and nudging her off my man. "It's never this one," I tell Cooper, my chest bumping up against his as I try to give us some privacy. "It's the fat one you gotta watch out for."

"You mean the one who looks like he's capable of murder?" Cooper nods up above my head to Tom "innocently" strolling across the pillows and leveling Cooper with a possessive stare. He plops on his hind legs and sets a paw atop my head.

I cover my face with my hand, closing my eyes as I giggle against Cooper's hard, hot body.

"Why'd you want them here?" he asks, raising an eyebrow.

"You do realize that this is what you should expect with *children*." I tilt my head in an arrogant know-it-all fashion that is probably not the most attractive thing. "Why do you think my brother needed a babysitter?"

He silently chuckles at my point. "There will be a lock on my bedroom door."

"And that will stop little fingers from appearing through the crack by the floor?"

"I'll kick a pillow over there." He flattens against me, eyes flicking to the cat for a brief second before he rests his head on the heel of his hand. "Kids don't prevent moments like these." His finger taps the tip of my nose. "That's how people have more than one."

It takes everything in me to bite back my retort. Moments like these don't happen to longtime couples. I can't think of a time that was drawn out and savored after the first month or so, even with those I considered steady boyfriends. My sister, who is all too eager to hand out details about her sex life, has yet to describe a moment like this one. It's all quickies and interrupted orgasms. Even Holland with zero little distractions running around—yet—says her love life has lost its luster.

I blink up to his beautiful blue eyes swimming in hope and happiness—a surprising childlike quality to a man who is such stable ground. A wave rushes over me, and I catch myself before tipping over. I could easily fall into him without thinking twice.

Tom shifts above me, and I reach up and gently shove him over, ignoring his low mewls. With both my fur babies on the floor, I run a hand over the scruff on Cooper's chin, goosebumps cascading across my ribs at the coarse, manliness of it. He watches me in quiet reverence, fingers clenching into the sheets by my hip, and I grin at the restraint he's showing. This feeling is the one I don't want to lose: feeling sexy, desirable, in control and losing control all at once. It's the primal urges, the fun and animalistic desire to lose yourself in intense pleasure from someone new. It's the curiosity, the mystery… it's reading a book for the first time, jumping at a surprise you didn't see coming, hopping on a rollercoaster and not realizing it has a an upside-down loop.

For all that adventure and anticipation buzzing under my skin, there's a trace of trepidation with Cooper that throws me off balance for a moment. Will sleeping with him ruin the excitement I have whenever I see his face, hear his voice, touch his skin? Will it ruin it like it ruined all the others? The thought is far more devastating than I expected, and my fingers still against his jaw as I let it all process.

His eyes swivel between mine, sensing that I'm having an overthinking moment. He grins, his dimple creasing underneath my touch, and reaches up to twine his fingers with mine. He presses light kisses to each one of my knuckles before letting go to smooth my hair away from my face.

"How long's it been?" he asks.

"Is it that obvious?"

He shakes his head. "Two years for me."

I choke on the air between our lips, and he chuckles.

"Don't act so surprised."

"But you're... you're..." I gesture to him as if that's explanation enough.

"Painfully awkward?" he offers, throwing me for a loop.

"Huh?"

He sighs, his breath surprisingly still minty from last night's brush. He trails a lazy hand up my side, nearly making me forget the conversation as my eyes roll back.

"Not everyone can tolerate my blurting problem." He looks down in amusement when I shiver in his arms at his light touch. "The last time I..." He waves over our intertwined bodies, a rush of red painting his cheeks. I notice for the first time that the mark Claire drew on him has faded. "She told me in not so many words that I was good to look at, but a pain to listen to."

"Ouch."

"It was fine," he says with a laugh. "Nothing I hadn't heard before."

"That's horrible."

His face contorts into something that I can only describe as skepticism laced with constipation. "You can't tell me that you weren't put off by it."

167

"By your no nonsense, skip the small talk conversations?" I playfully pinch the skin near his elbow. "If I was put off by it, I wouldn't be here."

"Oh you got the full blast of it," he says. "My damn tongue ran away with me during that brunch."

"That's not normal for you?"

He shakes his head. "Not after she said that. I tried to back off, not come on so strong, but everything felt so... on the surface. Dates never led into more than a goodnight kiss because I never felt like I could get to know the girl. I *like* deeper conversations. I like knowing where she stands, what she sees for her future. I like peeling away at the layers that really mean something. I told myself that if I was going to be with a woman, I wanted to know more than just the surface."

"Funny coming from the man who kissed a woman after she only spoke two words to him." I give him a look, and he tosses his head back and laughs. With a playful growl, he curls back into me and hides his face into the pillow I'm resting in.

"I didn't say I was a purest." His voice muffles next to my ear. "Every man meets a woman who is the exception to his self-imposed rules."

A rush of warm butterflies soar through my midsection, and I blink at the ceiling, wondering if I've heard him correctly. Never have I been the exception. Never have I been anything but just another girl.

I coax him back up above me. "Please keep saying everything on your mind."

"It's not painfully awkward for you?"

"You have no idea how much your blurting problem turns me on."

"Well… damn. Maya, I think my tongue is about to run away from me again."

He lowers his mouth over mine, his tongue slipping between my lips. I sink into his kiss, my body already willing to take control over my thoughts. The fingers he was so gently caressing my skin with curl into my ribs, causing a harsh shiver to run up my spine and a gasp to fly out between our mouths. He gives me a satisfied grin before delving back into the kiss, tasting every corner of my mouth as I sink more and more into the sensations of his body, his touch, his skilled hands that I have a hard time believing are two years out of practice.

He moves suddenly, taking me with him as he sits us up. His touch is gentle against my face, yet aggressive on my waist, telling me he's skilled in both areas of physical expression. I can't stop the giddy, anxious giggle that sneaks out between our kisses.

As tentative as I am, I'm by far more eager to jump into the unknown waters of this complicated relationship. My fingers curl into the hem of his t-shirt, pulling at the material to get it up and over his head. It gets caught at all the right spots—abdominals, pectorals, biceps… yum, yum, yum. Laughter escapes us both as I get frustrated and turned on all at once by his muscular torso.

The cotton *flumps* against the floor, the static making his blond hair stand up. I smile and run my fingers through

169

the strands, giddy from the conditioned softness. My teenage fantasy about doing it with a beach blond is about to come true.

His eyes wander over my face as I trail my hand down his cheek, scrunching my nose at the adorable lines in the corners of his eyes. There are tiny grays sprinkled through the hair just above his ears, and I bite away a grin at them. My first gray hair was responsible for the Hershey massacre a year ago. His grays, however, cause my stomach to dive into another round of jitters.

My fingers fall to his collarbone, over his strong shoulders, squeeze his pectorals and scratch through his hairy chest. An uncontrollable squeal escapes me, effectively ruining any composure I may have been possessing.

His lips turn up, and he says, "Your turn," and a torrent of nerves rush through my midsection. My body is not something one ogles and gawks at. I'm a "do it in the dark" kind of person, and as the sun streams in from the windows, I get an electric shot of hesitancy that I'm not sure I'll recover from.

Cooper's fingers dip under my top, and I clamp my eyes shut, terrified of the expression I'll see on his face when he notices just how many rolls cover my stomach, or how low my bosom droops without the support of a push-up.

My knees bend out of habit, and I fold myself up hoping to cover what so many people view as flaws. The rush of cold air hits my back as it's exposed, and the sound of my shirt joining his on the floor floats past my ears.

"Mmm," Cooper moans, the sound coming from deep

in his throat before his lips are on mine once again. His hands which have been so focused on my face are now everywhere else. My shoulders, my elbows, my ribs, over my love handles, across my plush belly. He snakes them up between my breasts, catching my chin, holding me to him, and I can't seem to breathe. My worries have been chased away with his touch, his aggression, with his sweet and powerful kisses.

My back hits the soft cushion of the bed sheets, the coolness a welcome contrast to the heat that is spreading throughout my body. Cooper takes a hold of my bottom lip, pulling it out and eliciting a moan from the back of my throat. His hands are at my bottoms, and his voice is as anxious and heady as my heart as he says, "Help me out, Maya," and I push off the bed, allowing him to undress me in a way we haven't yet together. Everything joins the growing pile on the floor, and my eager hands go for his bottoms, and when I can no longer reach, I use my toes to push them down his toned legs. He laughs when they get stuck on his ankles, and I join him in his hormone-laced amusement as he fights with his clothing.

"You're covered, right?" I ask when he's back to kissing a path down the length of my neck. I fight the urge to thrust my hips against his before knowing if he brought a raincoat for the hot summer storm.

"Probably," he says, unconcerned. I push against the surge of pleasure striking at my core as his lips press to my hardened nipple.

"I'm… I don't have anything," I say breathlessly,

gulping hard to keep my head. "No kids. No kids, Cooper. We need something."

He chuckles into my cleavage before pressing hot, open-mouthed kisses on the unattended breast. "Relax, Maya. I'm not trying to trap you into a long term relationship with me." He winks before going back to giving me scorching pleasure.

"I… you… it's working, though," I try to tease, but I can't find the flirtatious voice in me anywhere. He's already trapping me with his tongue, his hands, his body, and I blink against the stars popping in my eyes, desperate to find some sort of ground to stand on so I can convey how very serious I am about birth control, but then his mouth is on my lower belly, and it feels too good to worry about anything. What was I thinking, anyway?

"Do you mind?" he asks, and I mutter something unintelligible which must've been a yes because his mouth is on me within the next second, and I jerk and buck against him. My head is up on a cloud and my heart is in a drum line, and I touch his hair, attempt to control my expletives, but they come out despite my best efforts to keep the cursing at bay. His tongue is a magician, and I'm a rabbit at his disposal. He's a cup of hot coffee in the morning and I am a drunken fool from the night before. My nails dig into the soft strands, and I hold on to the only anchor keeping me from floating off into the heavens.

"Up," I say, the only word that I can find after plummeting back to earth. "Up here."

He grins, holding a single finger to me before putting

way too much distance between us. My foggy vision is somewhat cleared as I watch his perfect, toned glutes disappear into the bathroom. My fuzzy hearing makes out the sound of his hands fishing around in a drawer, a box tearing open, a thunk of something hitting the bottom of a trashcan. He's back before I get a grip on myself, and a grateful smile plays on my lips when I notice the condom.

"No baby," he assures me, a glint settling in his dark blue eyes before he settles between my legs. Too anxious to wait for him, I grasp his taut rear-end and thrust myself up. If he planned on going slow, that plan is shot out the window the moment we're together.

He rocks into me, slamming harder and harder, faster and faster, and I'm gone yet again, starry-eyed and screaming out into a pillow I press over my face to muffle the sounds of the purest pleasure I've ever experienced. A cool wave of air rushes over me when Cooper rips the pillow away, tossing it into the unknown space around us. He presses his slick forehead to mine, groaning naughty words in my ear, pushing kisses to my lips.

Ten seconds, ten minutes, ten years later, he stiffens above me, and I reach up and push away his sweat-sprinkled hair, mind drifting down and floating into a moment of pure shock that this gorgeous man has just had sex with me.

He smiles around his panting, opening his eyes to mine. I blink, double-taking to make sure I'm not imagining the stars settled in his blue irises.

"Thank you," he says, withdrawing his hips. An unexpected pout pulls at my bottom lip as we separate. He smirks and playfully tugs at it before leaning back on his knees. "That was fun."

I know he probably says it so I don't get the wrong idea, but as he disappears to go take care of the birth control that I basically freaked on him about, a tidal wave of sorrow fills my chest, pushing tears up to the back of my eyes. I don't understand the response, because "fun" is the perfect adjective. That's what I wanted—*fun*. Nothing more.

Yet, as I reach for the sheets to cover up, that description of what just happened doesn't quite do it justice. It doesn't do Cooper justice. It doesn't do *us* justice... and now I'm thinking that there really could be an "us."

A groan rips through my throat and I roll my face into the sheets. So much for convincing him on the single life of flings and fun. I'm going to have to convince myself back into it first.

17

Gas and Cats

"Don't tell Warren I ate the entire basket of cheese fries myself."

Holland pushes the empty red burger tray to the center of the table, her belly popping the buttons on her shirt. Whether that's from the food baby or the actual baby, I'm not sure.

I zip a finger over my lips and then swirl my straw around in my strawberry lemonade. With it being a slow day for showings and Cooper stuck in the dentist's chair, I called up Holland for some much needed girl time. If anyone can convince me that the grass is definitely greener on the single side, she can. Pregnant Holland has a tendency to forgo the sugarcoating.

Her forehead bunches as she shifts, and her hand flies to her bulging stomach. I tilt my head and stop playing with my straw. "You okay?"

She nods. "Uncomfortable a lot lately. Been cramping on this left side." Her eyes try to smile through a wince.

"You think cramps are bad now…" She makes a horse rumbling sound with her lips, and I try to laugh away my concern. It doesn't work too well.

"Maya, I'm okay. I have a doctor's appointment day after tomorrow. Occasional cramping is normal."

Point for Holland. I nearly reach out and thank her for being so blunt about the cons of pregnancy. I take the nugget of information and pile it behind a locked door in my head that I'll unleash next time Cooper has his hands on me.

Her phone buzzes against the table, and she cradles her belly as she leans forward to grab it. She blows out another horsey sigh and types a text back.

"You have plans tonight?" she asks, her eyes only briefly leaving her screen before focusing back on the message she's sending. "Warren picked up another overtime shift."

I pause to think about the answer to that. I don't have any set plans, no, but staying with Cooper seems to be a standing date. Maybe he'll be okay with Holland hanging out. We are "married" after all. Not every night is dedicated to each other. See Exhibit A sitting across from me.

And while I'd rather spend another night alone with Cooper, it's probably wise to have a buffer when my feet are tiptoeing the line I was sure I wouldn't cross.

"Let me check with Cooper. You can come play in the mansion." I grin over my phone, holding back my amusement that we're both chatting with the men in our life when we wanted to spend some time just us girls.

I slide the phone back into my pocket, knowing Cooper won't answer for a bit since he's currently getting fit for a crown. Holland's back straightens in hopeful surprise at my offer.

"There's a pool, right?" she asks. "I could really go swimming right now. Feel weightless in this bloated body for once."

I hold back a snort and nod, handing off the bill to the waitress when she walks by. Holland and I have a trade-off system, and it's my turn to pay. Usually she's a little more frugal with her menu choice, but I was happy to see that she finally indulged in both an appetizer and an entrée.

Her wince is back, and she runs a hand over her stomach and holds her side, breathing as if she's in the third trimester and not the first.

"You sure you're all right?"

She nods at the table. "Promise. I'm not bleeding. I've read that this is completely normal."

Her words are in total contradiction to her tone, and after the pain passes she shakes her head at the empty food tray in front of her. "Damn it, don't tell Warren that he's probably right about my food intake. Next time I'll lay off the grease."

I chuckle, hoping that the action erases the unsettling feeling I have digging a hole in my gut. The waitress hands me back my card and wishes us a good rest of the day, and I shake myself into taking Holland's word over her health. She already has one worrywart hovering over her; she definitely doesn't need another.

My phone goes off just as I'm adding up the tip, and I let my brow pull in as I read the message.

"Cooper's done early," I relay to my friend. "I better get him back to his place and I'll see you there tonight?"

"Yes," Holland says on an exhale. "Thank you. Another night alone and I will go stir crazy."

I laugh, humoring her, but also stocking yet another tidbit away as ammunition when Cooper has me near ready to commit to him. Warren's been working so much lately that he's mostly gone and when he is around he's too exhausted to be entertaining company. I feel for my friend, and I give her a tight hug before parting. Yes, both of us could use a night to give our heads a break.

***

"Wheeeeeeeeeew!" Cooper hollers, pressing the down button on the passenger window of his precious truck. He stops it halfway down and then grins in stupid fascination as he rolls it back up.

"Someone's enjoying their laughing gas," I say, trying not to get too distracted by him as he tests all the buttons within arms' reach.

"Did you know," he says forcing a serious look on his droopy lips, "that my first client was a used car place?"

"I did not."

"Yeah." His eyes widen. "They paid us five hundred bucks to shoot a commercial. We couldn't hire actors so Robbie and I did it." He leans in further as if it's a big secret he's been keeping from me. "It was a local commercial that someone messed up in the schedule or something, and it aired during the Super Bowl. Wham bam boom, now I'm a billionaire. You knew that, right?"

"I am your realtor," I say, biting back my laughter.

"Mmm," he mutters, smile tilting his lips as much as it can through the Novocaine. His head falls against the headrest and he taps the ceiling of the cab. "Funny… people tell me I have it all. But I don't have what I want. Can't exactly buy a wife and kids."

"Sure you can," I tease, nudging him with my elbow. "You could probably throw a rock and find what you're looking for. You're a billionaire, easy on the eyes, funny, smart, charming, witty. You're basically the whole package. I'm surprised you haven't taken the first girl to come a knockin' and slap a ring on her."

"Maybe I'm looking for the whole package, too. Someone funny, witty, easy on the eyes, doesn't care about my money, preferably because she makes her own. She's content, strong, and smart, and I don't want to spend a day without her. I don't want just any wife and kids. I want *my* wife and kids."

How is he so profound while he's high as a kite? Perhaps some of that laughing gas has made its way over to me, because while a sentence like that would normally have sent me running, I almost feel like clinging on to him, hoping to prove myself worthy of just one of those qualities he's searching for.

He lets out a long sigh and rolls his head toward me. "If only you were up for the job. People think I'm lucky?" He snorts. "I'd give up every penny just for the chance at a future with you."

Yes, he's definitely reached the nonsensical point in his

pain medication. "Okay," I tell him, pulling up to the house and shutting the truck off, "I think it's time for a nap. Your tongue is starting to run away with you."

"I thought you liked that." He waggles a pair of suggestive eyebrows, and I fail at keeping my laughter at bay.

"Come on." I help him from the truck, his weight having an arousing effect on me as he drapes an arm over my shoulder. My hand holds onto his waist, and I can't help but appreciate the muscle under my fingers even with him resting his head on mine and gazing at me as if I'm something to be treasured.

"You're so beautiful," he murmurs as we step up the front porch. "I like this freckle you have right here."

His finger presses into my cheekbone much harder than I expect, and I jerk back with a laugh. We get inside and I take one look at the staircase and opt to set him down in the sitting room instead. He *flumps* down into the cushions, laughing as he does so. His cheeks are puffy and his eyes are crossed. He looks out of his mind, and yet I still find him sexy as hell.

"Time to sleep this off, my friend," I say, pulling a woven blanket up over his shoulders. As entertaining as he is, I hope the effects have worn off by the time Holland gets here. I'm already worried about Cooper's lack of filter while he's sober; I can't imagine the ribbing I'll get if his laughing gas pairs up with my best friend of ten plus years.

His eyes close almost instantaneously with the drapes when I pull them shut, casting the room in darkness. I grin at his deep breathing moving his chiseled chest up and down, his lips parted and his face half into the pillow. There is a foreign emotion nibbling at my heart, making it twitter beneath my fingers as I press them to my chest in a sore attempt to calm the chaotic beating. I'm attracted to Cooper. I think he is amazingly sexy and I am aroused by his wit, his honesty, his touch, his eyes, his hair, his smile. I'm familiar with those responses. I can put words to them, know how to react when they make an appearance. But this one... I'm at a complete loss. I want to sink into his mind and feast on all of his thoughts. I want to be close to him when physically close isn't close enough.

I try to shake myself out of these thoughts, rip my eyes away from his sleeping form on the couch, and focus on the things that I know I want. One person for the rest of my life is a terrifying thought. Pregnancy, children, making choices that affect so many other people and not just myself... I'm not used to that. I'd bet I'm no good at it either. But for the first time ever, I can envision that kind of life with Cooper, and it doesn't entirely make me want to run away.

After creeping from the room, I head back outside for some fresh air, and hopefully some fresh perspective.

***

The sun is hitting the point in the afternoon when it colors the entire house orange. My cats have finally braved exploring the rest of the place and have spread themselves to their absolute tallest across the sitting room floor. The daylight shines across Tom, making his coat look like he dove into a tube of lubricant. Kat is flat on her back, paws in the air, soaking up the rays. I close the book I'd been trying to get lost in and frown at them both.

"Traitors," I mutter under my breath. They were my excuse when it was time to go back home. Cooper has been hinting in his sleepy daze that he wishes I would stay longer than two weeks. Tom and Kat were supposed to continue their grumpiness so I don't weaken if and when Cooper asks me in all seriousness.

Speaking of, a low groan rumbles from the couch, and the owner of that panty-dropping sound slowly shifts onto his back. His arm lifts to his jaw, his fingers running across trimmed scruff.

"How big was it?" he asks, eyes opening to my questioning brow. "The truck that hit me."

I let out a small laugh. "It was more like a drill."

"Or a jackhammer." He lets go of his jaw and eases himself to a sitting position. "Would you do me a favor and grab me some Tylenol? It's in the bathroom cabinet."

I nod and pad my way across the open floor plan to the guest bathroom under the vast staircase. After tipping three pills into my palm, I tilt a crystal glass under the faucet and bring him both. The lift of his brow at the water and the flash of gratitude in his eyes bubbles my stomach with a sense of usefulness I haven't quite felt before. I haven't experienced being in a responsible roll where I actively and willingly take care of someone other than myself and my cats. I kinda like it.

"Thanks," he says then pops the pills and takes a generous gulp of water. I offer to put the glass back, but he sets it on the table behind the couch. He gestures for me to join him, and I slump down, instantly warming from our touch combined with the sun streaming through the crack in the drapes.

His eyes roam over me, and because my mind is still tumbling with thoughts I don't want to have, I stay quiet. He drops his hand over mine and mindlessly plays with the bracelet dangling from my wrist.

"Another favor?" he asks.

"Hmm?"

"Forgive me for whatever I said while under the influence?"

I laugh. "You said nothing incriminating."

"Then why the long face?"

"Tired." It's sort of the truth. "Thinking too much maybe."

"About…?"

Us. The word is on the tip of my tongue, but I can't find the courage to say it. Voicing it only makes it so much more real.

My gaze drifts over our legs touching in so many places, our bodies so comfortably pressed together. It almost seems unreal. So unreal that I can hardly believe it will last, even if I wanted it to.

His quiet laugh breaks me out of my head, and I meet his eyes as he says, "Yeah… you definitely are."

"Huh?"

"Thinking too much."

I push him lightly in the arm, and he winces, but not from my touch. His hand is back on his jaw. Grateful for the

183

temporary distraction, I take the opportunity to wildly change the subject.

"You know what you need?"

"Blow job."

I roll my eyes at his very male response, giving him the benefit of the doubt; he's probably still coming out of the gas. "No." I wave my arm out at my fur babies. "A cat."

"That is the last thing I need."

I shake my head. "Cats are a great source of healing power."

He tilts an eyebrow at me, and I push his legs so that I can snag Kat before she runs away. She's not the best cuddle-bug, but she's less of a butthole than Tom. With Cooper's trepidation, I'm going with the nice one, because they both have claws.

The orange ball of fur flinches with surprise when I wrap my hand around her belly and cradle her to my chest. She goes from sleepy to tense in my arms the closer I get to Cooper, and I sense that she's only matching his emotions. His blue eyes are wide and worried as I settle the kitten in his lap.

She's there for less than a second before she takes off and hides.

"I'm cured!" Cooper teases, and I wrinkle my nose at him before reaching for the large cat I have to use two hands to get up off the floor. Tom lets out a low growl as I move him from his sunny spot, but he's otherwise still just as lazy as he was before I disturbed him.

"Try this one."

"That one will kill me."

I level Cooper with a look and plop Tom down a little harder than I planned. After getting the wind knocked out of him from the weight, Cooper makes a sound similar to Tom's growling as the old cat curls up for a nap.

"Pet him," I instruct, stroking down Tom's hot black fur. "The purring starts the healing process."

"You read this on the internet or something?" he asks, that skeptical eyebrow still raised sky high at me.

"Yes."

"Oh!" he says just as my pocket vibrates. "I get it. You're crazy."

"Pet him," I say again, seeing Holland's name on my screen. "I'll be right back."

I hold in a laugh as a look of panic flashes in Cooper's blue irises. His fists stay firmly at his sides while he doesn't move a muscle underneath Tom's weight. I wickedly wiggle my eyebrows as I leave the room and answer my phone.

"Hey," I say through a laugh to Holland on the other line.

"Hey."

My amusement is gone, my heart stopping mid-beat at the wetness in her voice. "What's wrong? Are you okay? Is Warren all right?"

She sniffs. "I'm fine. Just disappointed. I don't think a swim is a good idea tonight."

"Sick again?"

"Oh yeah." She gulps. "Sorry. I really needed it, and then..." She drifts off, groaning.

185

"Do you need me to come to you?" I offer. I really don't mind it, though the thought of leaving Cooper on one of the few nights I have left with him is a little more gut-wrenching than I thought it'd be.

"It's not pretty, Maya."

"I've seen you puke before."

"Don't remind me." Her soft laugh floats through the phone. "I'll be fine. Just want to sleep and be alone for a bit to wallow in my misery."

"You sure?"

"Uh huh."

"Let me know if you change your mind."

"I won't. Enjoy spending time with that sex god you're staying with. Seriously. I'd like to live vicariously through you."

I bite away a grin, my cheeks warming at the reminder of Cooper's very capable hands all over my body. Sex god, indeed.

"Feel better. Love you."

"Love ya, too."

My thumb swipes the red button left, and I let out a long sigh of relief that my suspicions were squashed. I wouldn't wish nausea on anyone, but better that than what I was thinking.

I turn around, and my feet stop in their tracks when I catch Cooper slowly running his hand over Tom's back. My grumpy butt cat is nudging Cooper with his head, his purring so loud I can hear it from across the room. A smile teases at the corner of Cooper's mouth, and something warm and winged rises in my chest.

"Feeling better?" I ask, leaning against the wall to gaze at the heart-fluttering view. Cooper's eyes flick up, narrowing slightly at the fact that he got caught.

"Not another word, Miss Baker."

18

Guarded Hearts

With Cooper's tooth fixed and his brain back to normal, the next few days pass by in a blur of work and sex. Twice now at the same time. It's my very sore attempt to try to prove to *him* that the fun part of a relationship is the sparkly first few days in. And when that doesn't work, I prowl around in a very sluggish fashion, being as unladylike and uncensored as possible. Last night when he caught me spitting an impressive amount of toothpaste and saliva into the sink, spraying the faucet and his hand, he just looked at me with those gorgeous blues and said, "You're adorable" and then wiped his hand off.

"Cooper," I breathe, my voice getting caught in my throat as a surge of pleasure courses through me. My hands trip over a table full of paint supplies as I try to keep myself from tumbling to the floor. "A condom, babe. We need a—"

"I know, I got it." He smiles against my lips, his hand snaking out from under my skirt to retrieve the foil package from his pocket. It takes me too long to realize I've uttered a

pet name at him, and by the time I feel like I should take it
back, he erases every thought I've ever had.

I think it's the only cure for the terrifying notion that
Cooper may just be the real thing I never wanted to find.
Whenever there has been a moment when I feel that
inexplicable emotion I can't put words to, I jump him, eager
to have my mind erased completely. This time… well, he
only asked me to meet him here so we could go to a showing
I set up for him. Instead I caught him in the middle of
splashing paint over a giant canvas in one of the side offices.
His eyes were dark and sad, and I instantly felt myself
swirling into sorrow with him without even knowing if there
was anything wrong.

Back when Julie first met Nathan, my mother asked her
how she could fall in love so quickly, how she knew it was
love that she felt. Julie told her that she feels everything
Nathan feels, wants everything he wants, needs him as much
as he needs her.

As that description started making more and more sense
looking into Cooper's sad eyes, I crossed the room and
brought his lips to mine before I could give it any more
thought. He didn't seem to mind in the slightest—in fact,
he's also in a much better mood.

"Hi," he breathes, his hand releasing the crook of my
knee now that we've both been to our peak and back.

"Hi."

"I'd say I'm happy to see you, but that doesn't
accurately describe it."

I smooth down my skirt. "Having a rough day?"

He nods, turning around to take care of his own wardrobe. "I found some fraudulent charges on one of our accounts. If it's who I think it is..." He lets out a long sigh, a soft smile somewhere in the worry lines of his face. "He's a good friend."

"A good friend doesn't steal from you," I point out, trying to be helpful, grateful once again for Cooper's straightforward personality; he can so candidly talk about what is bothering him. I do not possess that particular quality.

"I know." He runs a hand through his hair. "I want to talk to Robbie first. See what he thinks."

"I can wait," I tell him. "The place I'm showing you is vacant. We can leave whenever you're ready."

He leans forward and presses a gentle kiss to my forehead, so contradictory to our hard and fast romp not two minutes ago. It throws me, because I can't help but appreciate how wonderful both displays of affection are.

"Actually... if you want..." He stops and shakes his head. "Never mind."

"What?"

"Well, this room was set up to get these canvases painted for an ad we're shooting. If you feel like playing around, that'd help us out."

I snort and let my eyes drift over all the different colors on the table my butt was up against. "I don't paint."

"Neither do I." He jokingly nods to the splash of blue he chucked at the far back, wall-length canvas. "Guess I'm a natural."

Before I can give him crap about his painting skills, he pushes a quick kiss to my lips and heads down the hall. I crook my neck, letting my gaze follow until he's no longer in sight. Poor guy. I know how it feels to have to fire a friend. And I set my hand to my heart and push away the sorrow that's starting to creep back in there. I'm only empathizing. Yes. It couldn't possibly be because I'm feeling what he's feeling just because I'm strongly attracted to him. Yet, it's the first time I've watched him leave a room without checking out his ass.

I shake my head, feeling ridiculous. He hasn't proved anything, really. Our experiment so far has been... *fun*. If this is his definition of a long term relationship, maybe I could handle it. Even taking him to the dentist wasn't boring in the slightest.

It's just because our relationship is young. I'm infatuated, is all. Infatuation: a foolish and extravagant admiration.

Yet, that word doesn't seem to fit.

I growl under my breath and head out the door, following in his footsteps. The urge to calm my ragged breathing is too strong to just sit and wait. He's worried, so I'm worried, and I'm not going to try to figure out why that is.

I stop when I hear Robbie's voice billowing from an open office door, and I rest against the hallway wall and try to look inconspicuous.

"Why are you even hesitating?" he says, and I hear a thick file hit a desk. "Fire his ass, then sue it for good measure. I'm about ready to get our lawyer on the phone."

"Whatever happened to giving people the benefit of the doubt?" Cooper says, his voice vibrating somewhere deep in my chest. "He's been with us for a long time."

"Probably means he's stolen way more than we should've let him get away with."

Cooper's quiet for a moment. "I know." He sighs. "I know, you're right, I just… this is gonna be messy. He's got a family. Little kids at home."

"Then he shouldn't have taken the risk. Damn it, Coop, don't get soft. We all got problems."

"It's not about being soft. It's about knowing all of that and still wanting to take him to court. It's about being his friend for years only to put him on the street. I wasn't like this. It's pennies to us, yet I want to ring his neck. What does that say about me? Firing him feels so… heartless."

Robbie chuckles, but that sound only guts me from the inside out. I clutch at my chest, push back the sting behind my eyes, and try to calm my breathing. No one has a bigger heart than Cooper, and to hear him talk so openly about how he feels he doesn't have one? It ruins me. I want to break down the door and assure him otherwise… and give Robbie a glare over his blasé reaction for good measure.

"You want to talk heartless, bro? Stealing from the guy who gave you a job… not just any job, but a lucrative career… now that's pretty damn heartless."

I drop my hand in the silence that follows, let it swing like a pendulum down by my side. This isn't my concern; it's Cooper and Robbie's and my opinions here don't matter.

My nose is buried deep into things I know nothing about, and I can't know any more about. Cooper and I are separate entities; he owes me no explanation and I owe him nothing when it comes to the day to day stresses. That is marital relations, serious couple talks, not for two people playing house. I force myself back to the canvas-filled office, trying to convince myself that I don't care.

It doesn't work. I care all too much, no matter how frightening that is.

***

A strip of light streams across the canvas, turning the colors I carefully selected into bright hues that completely contrast. I chuckle at the painting, brush poised between my thumb and forefinger. A blue droplet falls onto my knuckle, and I let it streak down to the back of my wrist along with several of its friends. I believe there is more art on my hand than made by it.

"Well, you can rule out painter for your retirement plan," Cooper says from the doorway.

I turn with a frown. "Don't like my interpretation of a midday horizon?"

"Oh, I do. Especially the signature."

My name resembles that of a kindergartner, scribbled across the entire bottom of the canvas in black. It covers the original signature in orange that was, believe it or not, much worse on the eyes.

He chuckles, pushing off the doorframe and wrapping his arms around my waist. "Thank you. I'll make sure it's in the back of the shoot."

193

"The way back."

I feel his smile on my neck, and based on touch alone, I know it's a lackluster grin.

I swivel in his arms. "You ready to go?"

"Just about." He pushes his forehead against mine. "I have one more conversation ahead of me, but… I had to see you first."

The words I overheard ping around in my head, and I let out a sigh and run a hand over his chest. He has no idea just how wonderful his heart is, how I wish I had one just like it.

I pull at buttons of his shirt, undoing just the top few to expose the white undershirt hugging his pectorals. Careful not to get any bit of his clothing, I tug the material down with one hand and hold it out of the way while I push the tip of the paintbrush against his chest.

The brush leaves a broken path along his skin, flecks of paint speckling his arm as I form the only shape I know how to paint correctly.

"What's this?" he asks, his lip crooked up in an adorable half-smile.

"A heart," I simply say.

"Yes…" He chuckles. "Why are you painting it on my skin?"

I let out a breath, pulling the brush away to study my work. "I would hate think that because you have to make some hard decisions today, that you start to doubt that you have one."

He meets my gaze, the amused glint in his eyes slowly

fading into something else entirely. The power behind his stare sucks the breath straight from my lungs, causing my heart to work that much harder to keep me upright.

"You heard?"

I lift a shoulder. "A little. You mad?"

His hand covers mine still poised near his chest, fingers weaving and making me lose my grip. The paint brush tumbles end over end to the floor, forever staining the carpet with this moment that somehow already feels significant. The small of my back warms with his touch as he pulls me even closer, our bodies melding in a comfort comparable to a warm bed on a cold morning.

He takes the first step into a soft waltz, and I follow his lead, grinning against his chest in a sweet realization that this is another thing I didn't believe I wanted, or would ever enjoy, yet I find myself wanting to stay under the covers, in a manner of speaking. Impromptu dancing to nonexistent music was more likely to happen in the movies, never to someone as unromantic as I am.

As I was…

My fingers tighten between his, and I leave the foreign emotion I feel in this moment unspoken, though I'm pretty sure I've discovered exactly what it is.

19

Love Bug

I flip to my side, blowing out a frustrated breath in the darkness. It's 2:30, and I haven't had an ounce of sleep. I never had this problem B.C. (before Cooper), but it seems a side effect of falling for the man is insomnia.

My hands flop onto the bed sheets, nothing disturbing either Tom or Cooper as they sleep soundly on the other side of the massive king-size. Mr. Grumpy Butt has set up camp alongside Cooper's bare back, stretched out so much that his front paws rest near Cooper's hip and his tail curls up over Cooper's upper back.

If Cooper woke up, he'd probably pretend to hate his new cuddle buddy, but I know better, and the realization that I know that much about him crashes into my stomach and makes it that much harder to sleep.

He's a stomach sleeper. His muscular back rises and falls with his heavy breathing and the comforter rests across his hips. If I wasn't afraid of waking him, I'd stroke a finger down the line of his spine and trace over the hills and valleys of muscle that cover his body. Imagining it alone has my thighs clenched together, but what's more concerning is the fact that it isn't his muscles at all that have my heart pitter-pattering and my mind refusing to shut down.

It's because when I touch him, he gets a twitch in the corner of his mouth that is so freaking adorable that it makes me want to touch him any chance I can get. It's the hopeful, childlike look in his blue eyes when I agree to whatever mundane task he's asked me to do for him. It's the word vomit he spouts at the most random of moments that make me blush and take my breath away. It's watching his nose wrinkle when one of my cats jumps up on his lap. It's the wince that pinches at his forehead when I stick my cold feet on him. It's the content and joy that rests in his eyes when he held my nephew, or when he had tea with my niece.

I reach out, but stop halfway to his back and quickly flip onto my other side. How did this happen? A couple weeks with him and a lifetime of views have flipped on its head. I push the comforter off of me, flinging Kat to Cooper's side of the bed and causing Tom to let out a low growl. I stand at the foot of the bed and wait, watching Cooper until I know for certain I haven't woken him up.

There's a smile on his lips, and he's totally snoring. He's even adorable while sleeping. Damn him.

I tiptoe across the carpet and sneak into the hallway. The house is so big, so quiet. It feels weird to me, suddenly, even though this was essentially my dream. Make money, buy a huge house just for me. No kids to make noise, no relationship outside of the one with my cats. A place to have cocktail parties—if that's even a thing anymore—or to entertain people, but mostly to just have all this space to myself. As I listen to the silence—minus Cooper's cute snores—that seems so… empty.

"But I'll travel," I whisper out loud, like I'm trying to convince myself that I haven't changed my mind. "I won't have to find babysitters or compromise on where I go and what I do when I get there. It's going to be so great."

But even putting a voice to it doesn't make it sound so great. Cooper's snoring isn't helping things either because suddenly I feel like I could listen to that sound every night for the rest of my life and *that* would be great.

I shake my head and start down the stairs, putting as much distance as I can between my ears and his snores. I need a wake-up call—some cure for the love bug bite. After rummaging through the fridge and cupboards and coming up with nothing that sounds good, I wander around the house, going from floor to floor, from room to room, arguing with myself the entire time.

When I step into basement and hear water lapping, I slip off my slippers and push open the door to the pool. The air in here is sticky and humid, but it clouds my head with thoughts of that instead of the other, so I already feel better.

The pool is surrounded by windows, all fogged from the heat rising off the water. I can't see any stars, the night sky either clouded over or the windows too foggy to see clearly through. I rub my arms, not from being cold—I'm very much the opposite even in my pajama shorts and cami—but to try to rub out the jittery feeling running under my skin. I've spent two weeks with Cooper here in this house, a house that is neither of ours, and as determined as I was that I wouldn't fall, I feel myself slipping off the edge. Thoughts of a future with him keep invading my mind, keeping me awake, making me equally excited and terrified.

I've been with other men for much longer, and never did I entertain the ideas that have been running wild in my head. I've found myself wondering what our house would look like someday, if I can convince him to build one, and then I shake myself out of it, shocked that my mind went in that direction so naturally. I've paused at wedding magazines in the checkout, doodled his name on Post-Its in my office, wondered about when I should let him meet the rest of my family.

And now, as I sit on the edge of the pool and dip my feet in the surprisingly warm water, the thought that enters into my head is that if I'm meant to have babies, I want them to be his babies.

I bury my face into my hands and try to breathe. For years I've argued my point, driven it home to all my family and friends who asked. It's okay to not want kids. It's okay to want to stay single. It's okay to have fun and live my life the way *I* want to live it. Admitting that I'm starting to see something different, *want* something different, feels like I'm admitting that I was wrong.

I don't think I was wrong at all. Some people don't want a family, and that's okay. But wanting a family isn't wrong either. Wanting the wedding, the house in the suburbs, the kids running wild... that's not insanity. It's not a false hope. It's just someone else's dream. And seeing Cooper want it so badly, and falling for him not despite it, but *because* of it, now makes it feel like my dream, too.

A low grumble escapes my lips, and I slide fully into the water, clothes and all, just to see if it'll jolt me back to the person I used to be. My head dips below the surface, and I try to sit on the pool floor, but I've never been much of a sinker; I bob right back up to the top. So I float around for as long as I can hold my breath.

As much as I want the water to make my mind shut up, now I'm chuckling to myself at the thought of Cooper trying to clean a pool by himself instead of letting a professional do it. No doubt he's tried before, if he has a pool in any of his numerous properties.

I don't think I want a pool. It seems a little scary, to be honest, not to mention the maintenance on one of these things. What if I forget to lock the door or something, and one of my kids finds their way into the water? My heart squeezes just at the thought, and then it jumps as if it just realized that I've pictured kids in my future again. Because honestly, I'd want a pool if it weren't for that.

So I guess I want a pool? Ugh, what has that man done to me?

I lift my head and take a deep breath before settling back into the water. I watch my clothes float around me, my hair curtain out on the surface. This is relaxing—maybe I should flip to my back and sleep here.

The water jostles around me, a flurry of bubbles popping right next to my body. Next thing I know there is a

arousing. I cradle his face in my hands, words never finding their way to the surface as I look into his eyes and hope and pray he can see my every thought. He covers my mouth in a seductive, hot kiss that sets my entire world on fire.

I'm in love with him. There is no falling—that part is done and over with. I'm deep in the pools of love and I don't ever want to crawl my way back out.

He pushes me up on the edge of the pool, his fingers tucking into my shorts and I frantically try to help him pull them off. He flings them behind him, and the land somewhere in the water as I scramble back along the floor, watching the water drip and pour off his muscular, lickable body when he pushes himself out. He drops his boxers, kicking them into the pool alongside my bottoms before he sticks his hand out for me.

I tuck my fingers in his palm, and I severely underestimated his strength. He pulls me to my feet, bends his knees, and a giggle escapes the back of my throat and echoes around us as he hoists me over his shoulder. I get a glorious view of his ass—and smack it for good measure—while he walks me over to the hot tub. Thank heavens we aren't walking too far away; I want him inside me asap.

He lowers me in the center, and for once in my life, I'm not too concerned about how much flab is going on. He doesn't mind it, and really… I don't think I do either. Not when he's looking at me like he is.

"Come here?" he asks, slowly sitting in the hot water and hitting the jet button on the side. I love that he asks, that he's a guy who knows what he wants, but respects what other people want, too. I slide onto his lap, slipping him inside as I settle.

I hate being on top. There was always that self-conscious bug that bit me every time. I'm too much boob, too much hair, and my cardio and stamina is not anything to write a book about. But I *want* to be on top now. I want to show him just how much he means to me. I want to keep that look on his face for as long as possible.

I rock my hips, the first satisfying rub sending a tingly flush under my skin. His own body is red, wet, and the steam rising around us only adds to my arousal. But it's the joy in his eyes, the loving caress of his fingers on my jawline that is making me feel so good.

I make love to him for a lifetime, yet not long enough. When I feel myself tumbling over the edge, throwing my head back in ecstasy, a small part of my mind is sad that it's almost over. Cooper is saying something, his voice muffled through the clouds in my ears. There's pressure on my hips, on my thighs, and as I blink myself into coherency, I realize he's pushing me from his lap, desperately shoving against the stone grip I had on his waist.

"Maya, I—"

I kiss him as hard and strong as I can in the aftermath of the orgasm. His hands are still urging me off of him.

"Maya," he says around my lips. "You've gotta… you have to get off."

My head is still foggy, and I grasp for the reason for his request. It can't be my weight, can it? I'm light in the water, and he picked me up without breaking a sweat.

But as he softens inside of me, the realization hits like a sobering bucket of ice water and I all but leap off his lap. We've been making love for so long that the jets have stopped, and I can see his release in the water. My heart trips and heat rushes through my cheeks.

"Maya…" he says, his eyes polar opposite from the joy that was in them not ten seconds before. He reaches out to me, and I easily go back to him, wanting to feel the comfort of his skin as my body starts to shake with panic.

"I pulled out as fast as I could," he tries to comfort me, but I can feel the evidence between my legs, and I don't know if its him or if it's just the hot tub water. "It's gonna be okay. I heard… I'm pretty sure you can't get… not with the hot water."

I shake my head against his, silently letting him know that I don't need him to comfort me with words. I don't want this moment ruined by a lapse in judgment. I press my lips against his, soft and gentle, but hard enough to let him know that I still have fallen for him, that this isn't going to change how I feel.

But I wonder if he can sense how scared I am now. I *never* forget a condom. *Never.*

He wraps his arms around me, and he pushes us up and out of the hot tub. We sit on the edge, wrapped up in each other until finally sleep takes me over.

20

Maybe Baby

My bathroom mat has been trampled down from fluffy to flat within the last twenty minutes. All I've done is pace and pace in my Cozy King pajamas and stare at the blue box on the counter, occasionally talking to myself.

It's been one week since I packed my bags and came home. One week since I Cooper and I made love in the hot tub. One week of tossing and turning every night before breaking down and begging him to come over just to sleep in my bed. He was so sweet about it, too. One night he showed up at around four, his hair disheveled and his eyes droopy. He pressed a sleepy kiss to my forehead and used me for a crutch as we climbed up my stairs and fell on the bed. He was out within a minute. I followed almost immediately after.

"It's okay," I tell myself for the tenth time. "It's fine. I don't feel sick, my boobs aren't sore, and I'm not experiencing any cravings that are outside of the norm. I'm just being paranoid."

Kat rubs up against my bare ankle, and I stop my pacing and lean against the counter. My mirror self looks like she's gone through the ringer, and I'm too fidgety to even try to fix my hair or adjust my clothes. It's not like I have to look like a rockstar to pee on a stick anyway.

"There's no signs of a bun in the oven," I tell myself again. "Well... other than the obvious one."

I'm only a day late, but a one day delay is one day more than I'd like, especially after my birth control brain fart.

I shift my weight onto my other leg, clenching them together a little to keep all the water and orange juice I drank in there until I get the guts to rip the box open. Okay... there are only two answers here. A negative result means I can breathe again. Cooper and I can have some fun in the new romance stage and I can slowly dip my toes into something more. I just got past my qualms about *that*. So a positive result would mean...

I swallow hard, hanging my head and watching Kat try to squeeze her way through my ankles. She's purring hard, and I wish I could say that was helping, but my nerves are way too shot to calm down even for a comforting kitty.

"Okay..." I say. Maybe speaking it out loud will make it sound better. "If it's positive, I'll go to the doctor and make sure. Just one step at a time. No panicking."

A rush of warm, heavy pressure plummets in my lower belly, and I jam a hand between my legs, but there's no stopping the force of a full bladder. My shaking hands fumble for the box, tearing it open and grabbing the stick, which is also in a wrapper. But with slick, sweaty fingers, a nervous heart and an overflowing bladder, I can't get the darn thing open. A hiss slips through my teeth as my thumb slips and slices on the wrapping. I start bouncing on the balls of my feet, biting the edge of the wrapper and tearing through it just in time for me to yank down my pants and let loose.

Hmm… maybe waiting until you're about to explode is the key to feeling relief when taking a pregnancy test.

My doorbell rings right in the middle of my business, and Kat runs through the open bathroom door and ducks under my bed. I hope it's just UPS.

As I'm setting the stick down on the counter and searching for a Band-Aid, the doorbell goes off again, followed by a few knocks. I let out a huff and check the box. Two to three minutes for results. Well, whoever's at the door has impeccable timing. I run a brush through my hair and jog down the stairs and peek out the peephole.

It's Holland… and she's running a hand over her cheek like she's wiping away tears. My fingers quickly close over my lock and flick it open.

"Hey," I say as I swing the door open. "What's wrong?"

Holland's red, watery eyes meet mine briefly before she drops them back to her feet. "I…" She sniffles and my heart plummets into my stomach.

"I… I left Warren."

21

Best Buds and Hugs

Holland brings her long, dark ponytail over her shoulder, playing with the ends of her hair as we sit with Tom and Kat on my couch. Her crestfallen face hasn't had a flicker of a smile on it in the past few hours, even when she asked me to make her laugh, tell her funny stories, do anything just to make her not feel so heartbroken. I couldn't, though. I didn't have an ounce of humor in me. So I got her one of my cats and silently prayed for her.

"I don't want to go home," she says, dropping her hand from her ponytail to Tom's fluffy back. "I don't want to face him."

"What happened?" I watch her shake her head. "Holland…"

"This pregnancy…" She gulps away another round of tears threatening in her eyes. "We've both just become such different people. We're mostly fighting, and I feel so sick and horrible, I just need someone to understand and all he does is pester and hover and I… need a break."

"How long of a break?" I ask. They've been together over ten years. Even though I've seen them fight and I've heard Holland complain about things losing their spark, I still believed they loved each other.

She lifts one shoulder, shaking her head, her mouth open like she's at a loss for words. I quickly lean forward, setting a hand on hers, her fingers unusually warm for her. Holland's always complaining about being cold.

"Why is he being so… controlling?"

"Do you know how long it took to get pregnant?" She brings her eyes up to mine, and I shake my head. "Four years."

"What?"

"We've been trying for four years."

My brow furrows, my brain trying to process. Holland and I tell each other everything. How did I not know about this? "I thought you guys wanted to wait ten years to have kids."

"I changed my mind." She sighs and starts stroking Tom's fur again. "When I told Warren I was thinking about starting earlier than planned, he was so happy. His eyes… seriously, Maya, I've never seen them sparkle like they did. Almost like he was just waiting for me to say it."

I shift uncomfortably on the couch, gaze drifting down to her baby bump. "Why didn't you tell me?"

She snorts, the first slip of amusement—however hollow it is—she's had since she walked through the door. "Yes, Miss Anti-Baby is going to be fully supportive of me changing my mind and becoming 'one of them.' I mean, I got enough grief over getting married so young."

The joke has a jolting sting to it that I don't expect, and it shocks straight into my heart and sends bolts of guilt through my stomach. Have I really been so anti-family that even my best friend feels like she can't talk to me about what she wants? I guess I never saw it that way, always thinking about it defensively. I grew up with the idea that family, love, babies and marriage was the ideal to live up to. That was the life that meant you'd be fulfilled and happy. So when it didn't happen for me, I built a life that *I* could be fulfilled and happy with. Any time someone asked "Are you seeing anyone?" "You think there's a ring coming?" "How many kids do you want?" and when I'd answer honestly, saying that I don't want kids, I don't want a husband, I'd get the followups. "Why not?" "Aren't you lonely?" "Kids are so different when they're your own." I grew tired of it. Every time someone brought up family or marriage I instinctively thought it was a way to get me to "see the light." Maybe I was a bit too hasty to accuse and a bit too vocal about convincing everyone how happy I was that I didn't realize just how rude and disparaging *I* was to *them* for their choices.

I scoot across the couch, knocking Kat off my lap and wrapping my arms around my best friend again. "I'm sorry," I tell her. "Please don't feel like you can't come to me about anything. I'll be happy if you want a hundred babies."

Her hands come up around my waist and squeeze back. "Thanks, but… I don't think I can move past this," she says, her voice wet. "I feel like the man I fell in love with has been

213

ripped away from me. How can I start a family with a stranger."

I don't have an answer for her, but Warren could be completely oblivious to how he's making Holland feel. Men usually are.

"You have to talk to your husband," I tell her, pulling back and looking into her eyes. "That man loves you."

"What if he doesn't?" And the look in her eyes tells me that she actually thinks that's a possibility. "It's getting bad, Maya. I'm not even sure if I…" Her hands circle her tummy, and she blows out a breath. "I'd hate to bring a child into a broken relationship."

I want to tell her how her relationship isn't broken… maybe a little bruised, but not irreparable. But whatever brought her here is too fresh in her mind that there is no way she can hear it. So instead, I pat her leg and offer her a can of frosting. It's not until she laughs and races to the bathroom that I remember the pregnancy test upstairs.

22

Broken Woman

The paper under my butt crinkles as I shift and tap a message to Holland. She stayed at my place until Warren called in a panic, wondering where she was. I haven't heard a word since, and I'm trying to be patient, but I'm worried about my friend and her husband.

I hit send, sleep the screen, then blow out a breath and look at the picture of a uterus hanging on the opposite wall. The first pregnancy test had one bright line, one very faded line. The second had one line, but then overnight it grew a twin. I figured I'd be safe and get a professional opinion.

"Okay," I tell myself as the nerves ping and pop in my stomach. "If it's negative, no harm no foul." And I ask about birth control methods that I don't run the risk of forgetting. My eyes swivel from the display IUD over to the take-apart pregnant, torso-only manikin. It has different sizes of a baby, like one of those Russian Matryoshka dolls, starting from peanut to watermelon. I rub my tummy mindlessly, the material of the hospital gown catching on my paper cut. If it's positive... what do I do? What's the next step? I think about the life I have and the life that it'd turn into and even though I pictured it the night that got me into this mess, it still terrifies me. I'm not a mother; I don't have the patience, the know-how, the strength that I see in my sisters, in my friends. Motherhood suits them, just like I know fatherhood would suit Cooper.

Something warm crawls through my chest, and the corner of my mouth twitches as I look at that plastic baby. "If it's positive, I tell Cooper." And we deal with this together. That's the next step.

A knock sounds at the door, and my spine straightens as the doc comes in. She's young, maybe my age, and I wonder if she has a family. And if she does, how does she juggle them and this?

"Sorry for the wait, Maya," she says, her smile friendly, but also like it's taking a lot of effort for her to keep it there. I'd chalk it up to an occupational hazard if it wasn't for that gut feeling that it's most likely the news she has to deliver.

"It's okay." I let out an awkward giggle-snort that instead of calming me, just makes my cheeks warm. "So... what's the verdict? Life sentence?"

My joke falls dead between us, even the doctor unable to muster up some laughter just to humor me. Her lips turn down, and she reaches behind her for the circular, rolling chair and wheels it toward the bed I'm perched up on. She gently takes a spot, her fingers delicate as they adjust her white coat. I brace myself for my life to change.

"You're not pregnant," she says.

There is a two second beat of shock, followed by a long, loud sigh of relief. *Not pregnant*, oh thank heavens. No harm, no foul, just like I said before. Next step is talking birth control, and then I'm going out for a strong drink.

I grin, the nerves in my stomach evaporating, and I start to relax, my body stiff and sore from the tense position I hadn't realized I was sitting in for so long.

"Gah… don't do that," I playfully chastise her, and her brows pull in. "The look on your face made me think I was dying or something."

Sympathy fills her eyes, and an uncomfortable itch invades my relief. "Maya, your bloodwork has me concerned."

"*Am* I dying?" I ask, partly joking, mostly panicking.

She lets out a tiny laugh, and I wish she would just spit it out so that I could stop having these emotional mood swings.

"No. But, there are some more tests I'd like to run."

"Why?"

Her lips press together, and she sets her clipboard on the counter behind her. She starts slowly, medical jargon getting tangled among words that I actually understand. The longer she explains, the emptier I feel—emptier than I've felt in my entire life. Am I understanding her correctly? My fingers twitch against the hospital gown, tickling my stomach that not three minutes ago had the possibility of carrying something in it, but now…

"You mean… I can't have kids?"

Her eyebrows push together, her eyes swirling with

217

concern for me, just another patient. "It's a very low possibility."

A dull thud rings through my chest. "How low?"

"Under one percent."

My world fuzzes around me. This wasn't on my list of outcomes. I don't know what the next step is. There's this empty pit growing inside of me that I can't explain. There is a black cloud over my head, a heavy onslaught of hail pelting down on my shoulders. My insides crumple and shatter, screaming out in a pain they can't feel. I don't understand, not one bit; I never wanted kids. I was so *relieved* when I found out I wasn't pregnant. How can I feel such crippling grief over something I never wanted?

I can't find the words, only an empty joke on my tongue about how God just knew that I'd mess up being a mother. The doctor's voice muffles through my fog about making sure with more tests, but I can tell it's just a formality.

She leaves, and I dress in a fog. My phone is buzzing against the crinkle paper, Cooper's face on the screen. And suddenly I'm no longer numb to the pain; it's not dull or aching, but sharp and fresh, slicing through my chest and burrowing under my skin. I clutch at my stomach, curl into myself, and sob into my palm. Oh god, Cooper… If losing the idea of children hits me like this, it would kill him.

Would he leave me then? Would he leave if he knew that it's not just that I don't want kids, it's that I will never have them?

Another sharp pain shoots through my chest, and I lose

it right there on the gyno floor. An image of me telling Cooper I'm pregnant a year, two, even three down the road hits me like a dream that will never come true. His face lit up and his arms around me. He's so happy to be a father that he's already getting the measuring tape, he's already kissing my belly, he's already planning on which room to paint, which sibling to name god-parent, whether or not to announce on Twitter. I never saw it before, never thought there was a good, joyful moment to be had in the midst of morning sickness, up-all-nights, and terrible twos. Now that image is darkened, and all I see is the heartbreak down the road. Cooper's holding a baby that isn't his. We're babysitting or at a christening or some random family event. He's so content with the baby, but there's an underlining sadness in his eyes that won't ever disappear. The sense of loss that he won't have one of his own because he fell in love with a broken woman.

I can't do that to him. There is a difference between being unwilling to change your view on things, and forcing him to give up his views because you *can't* change. It's hope that the love that you have for each other will allow for some compromise. There *was* hope for a future family. He nearly had me convinced. But now, there's a "less than one percent" chance of that happening.

My butt hits the hard floor, and I hide my face in my knees. I know what the next step is now, but I'm not sure if I have the strength to do it.

23

Goodbye Cry

Cooper's laughter jostles my head resting on his chest, and I sneak a peek at his face in the light of my TV, his smile lines beautiful, his five o'clock shadow dark and in such contrast to his blond mess of hair on top of his head. I won't be able to look at him when I tell him. Those blue eyes have never been able to hide how he really feels—not to mention his mouth can't hide it that well either. One of the many reasons why I fell so hard so fast.

The room darkens as the screen goes from show to Netflix menu, and Cooper starts flicking through the choices.

"You up for another episode, or you want to watch something else?"

I lift a shoulder against the warmth of his underarm. I can't believe that I'll miss this. A month ago I would've traded any of my other suitor's just to cuddle with my cats instead.

My eyes drift to Tom who is giving *me* the evil eye for

taking up lap space when he hopped up on Cooper first.

"You're quiet tonight," Cooper says, selecting the next episode and setting the remote down. "You okay?"

No. "I… I have to talk to you."

His brow furrows, and he shifts enough that I get the full blast of concern swimming in his eyes. "What'd I do?"

I bite away a laugh at his joking tone, an ache pulsing in my chest at the fact that this is the last time we'll be light and fun with each other. I want to drag it out, soak it up before I have to break his heart.

"Lots of things," I tease, settling back down on his warm chest and staring at the TV. "But that's not what I need to talk to you about."

"Care to fill me in?"

"I'm working my way up to it." I snuggle into his shirt, smile turning upside-down as I remember him using the same line on me a few weeks ago. He was so nervous to ask me to stay with him—rightly so, I might add—but I bet he had no idea how hard I'd fall, how much he'd come to mean to me in such a short time, and how we should've walked away before it got to this point.

I can feel his grin through the kiss he places on my head; he must remember that day, too. "I'll prepare myself for random word vomit."

"I'm not as good at it as you are."

"The ol' Cooper bait and switch."

"Effective."

"Apparently. Next time I need to get you to do something you don't want, I'll just be quiet for an eternity and then blurt it out at the most inopportune moment."

"We need to stop seeing each other."

"You like my randomness and you know it."

"No, Cooper." I sigh and lift my head, begging my tears to stay inside where they belong. "We need to stop seeing each other."

His playful smile slowly fades. His light eyes darken. His breathing stops and starts back up in a puzzled rhythm.

"What?"

That one word… one word that doesn't mean anything and yet means everything—the beginning of the end. There's already so much heartache in that one word that I'm not sure I can continue. I want to laugh and say, "Got ya!" and snuggle my way back onto that strong and loving chest, tangle my fingers with his, kiss away every ounce of sadness and loss that is eating its way through my stomach. I slam my eyes shut and turn away, pretending it is someone else, someone I'm not so in love with, just another someone in a sea of someones who meant so little to me.

"I can't—" *No.* I don't want him to know. Or maybe I don't want to know how he'd react. I lick my lips and backtrack. "I don't want kids, Cooper."

He gives me a funny look, like he doesn't understand why this is such big news. "I know."

"I'm never going to… want kids."

"Maya," he says, his tone relaxing. "We're having fun right now. You wanted that, right?"

"I *did*—"

"You took a big leap with me. Playing house and giving

me a chance." He takes my hand, and a heavy tear pokes at the corner of my eye as I look down at our interlaced fingers. "Look, I know we want different things right now, but I'm willing to risk my future just for the chance to be with you."

"Don't say that."

"It's the truth."

"Cooper…" I want to draw my hand away, and I dig into the deepest parts of my strength to do it. I'm out of breath when I finally do. "We're too different, and I can't keep letting this play out when I know how it'll end."

"What makes you so sure it's gonna end at all?"

"Picture your life with me, okay? Picture it the way that it *will* happen if we stay together." I level my eyes, make sure that through all the fantasies he sees, all the dreams he has, that he can focus on the reality I'm going to paint for him. "You will *never* have children. Could you really live with that? Because I don't think I could live with taking that away from you."

And then I see it—his entire face falling as my words hit him. The pain that flashes in his eyes as the image becomes clear in his mind. The unshed tears of never holding his own baby, never teaching a son to ride a bike, or having date nights with a daughter. It's only me and him, and while for some people it's enough, for some people—like me—it *has* to be enough. But for him, it will *never be enough.* I could never give him what he needs, and I shove from the couch, pad my way across the room and bury my face in my palm, too afraid to feel everything I know he feels with just the *idea* of no family, when the reality is so very much mine.

"If I painted you a picture of what I saw for us, would it... would it hurt you as much as yours hurt me just now?"

"What?"

He stands, his footfalls heavy as he steps up behind me. He runs his hands down my arms, squeezing my elbows. "If I told you I picture a house with a big backyard, a swing set, a little girl with her mom's freckles and a little boy with her quick wit... would it hurt you?" His hot breath cascades over the back of my neck. "Maya, please look at me."

I slowly turn in his arms, knowing that he'll misinterpret the pain in my eyes for something I don't want instead of what it is—something I can't have.

"Are you sure you don't ever want that?" he asks. "Or even think that you could try to want that?"

I gulp, trying to keep my voice steady, but it's near impossible. "You said... you said you weren't trying to change my mind. You told me that was not what this"—I wave my finger between the two of us—"was about."

The shock of our conversation, the attempt to talk me back up falls from his expression, and he *crumples* in front of me. He reaches out, touching my arms, my hands, my waist... cupping my face and dragging his thumbs across my lips.

"This isn't happening, is it?" he says. "I feel like we aren't coming back from this."

I reach out for him, but draw back, knowing that if I try to cling onto him that I won't ever let him go.

"Would you be willing to give up kids for me?" I ask, not wanting an answer. Whatever it is wouldn't change anything. A yes would only triple my guilt over never being able to give him what he wants. A no would break my heart in a million ways.

His silence is just as earth-shattering.

"Then we have to stop this now, please." I sniff, a sharp pain slicing through the back of my throat from choking back all my tears. Cooper shakes his head, taking my hand and putting it to his lips.

"I don't think I can," he says. "You have become so much more than just the beautiful woman I saw on the street. So much more than my savvy realtor. So much more than the crazy cat lady."

We both let out a sad laugh at his words, and he takes my moment of weakness to step into me, hold me close, pattern kisses over my cheeks and across the bridge of my nose. "I don't want to let you go."

It takes every ounce of strength I have to push away, to coax his hands from my skin, to replace his warmth and comfort with something cold and lonely. I take a step back, my stomach tossing in a whirlwind of heavy, thick tar, my voice a distant cousin that I don't recognize. "I won't have kids," I say, knowing my words are carefully chosen. "I'm not going to change my mind, and… I don't want to change yours."

His eyes break again, his voice cracking and shattering my heart in two. "This can't be it. This can't be how it ends between us."

"Please… please go." I slam my eyes shut, but I can feel him a breath away again, closing the gaps between us and

225

filling it with his comforting body heat. "Cooper, please just go." He needs to go. He needs to leave before I tell him the truth, before I give in and marry him on the spot. I can't take away a family from him. I won't.

His hands are suddenly, softly on my cheeks; the warmth spreads from his palms and sinks into my skin. He taps a gentle kiss against my lips, a kiss that doesn't feel like his many others—the kisses that were persuading and meant to snare me into a moment of weakness. No, this kiss is warm and loving, kind and understanding, saddened and afraid.

"I'm sorry for lying to you," he says as our lips part. "For stupidly assuming everyone wants what I want, for trying to change your mind when I said I wouldn't. I wouldn't dream of asking you to give up anything just for me." He puts his forehead against mine, breathing in, inhaling like I'm inhaling, like we don't want this to end, that we'd both like to bask in it forever.

His eyes open to mine, the dark pools so unbelievably heartbroken and hurt that I nearly tell him to forget everything I've said. "So… I'm gonna walk away, but it is *not* because I don't love you."

He presses a long, lingering kiss to my forehead, drawing back so suddenly that I don't see his face before he turns. He slips into his shoes, not giving me a second glance as he pulls open the front door and steps out into the starry night. The *click* of the door as it shuts in place behind him sets off the flurry of tears I've kept just under the surface. I plummet to the floor, grasping at anything warm and soft to press my face into. Now I've lost both things I never wanted, and it's more devastating than anything I've ever experienced.

I didn't ask him to leave because I didn't love him, and I wish I would've said that before he walked out.

24

Missed Kiss

"Maya, you have a call on line three."

I run a hand over my forehead, hoping that I can rub out the little drummer boy who's made a permanent home there.

"Take a message?" I ask Sarah. "I think I'm gonna head home."

The corners of her mouth turn down, and her lips part like she wants to tell me whatever thoughts she has on my sour mood, but she thinks better of it and ducks out of my office.

It's been a painfully long twenty-seven days of seeing Cooper and not being able to touch, kiss, or tell him how I really feel. And he seems in just as much pain as I am, jaw always ticking as we wander around houses, like he's holding back everything and nothing all at the same time. Each showing ends the same—Cooper finding one imperfection with the place and asking if I know of anywhere else. Part of me wonders if he's truly dissatisfied or if it's a roundabout way of spending more time with me. We have another appointment in a few minutes, and I'm about ready to tell Sarah to take the lead on it. It's become more painful than exciting to see Cooper and help him pick a house he wants to start a family in.

The message light on my cell blinks, and my fingers slip off my drawer handle as I try to get some aspirin in me. He's early again. Always early. It's probably the only thing we have in common, aside from the fact that we're absolutely and totally in love with each other.

I quickly toss back the Advil and wash it down while clacking a response to Cooper. This better be the house he wants. Then it's very little face time until he signs everything.

"Maya?" Sarah says, poking her head in so cautiously I start to wonder if she's caught me crying or throwing things one too many times. "Mr. Sterling's here."

I push my drawer shut. "Feel like doing a showing for me?"

She humors me with a laugh, but she shakes her head and crosses the room. Her hands clasp around my wrists, and she pulls with all her might to get my mopey butt out of my chair.

"Think Cabo," she says, fixing my blazer. "Warm sand and blue drinks and no drama."

And no Cooper. Ugh, now all my dreams of traveling and beaches involve not some random islander, but a particular blond-haired, blue-eyed hunk of a man with a solid gold heart.

I let out a long groan, and Sarah says, "No, no... we're going to pull ourselves together." She ignores my frowny face and reaches up to fix my hair and makeup. Even if I didn't know her, I'd know she was a mom with the way she's handling me with equal amounts of tough love and concern. A soft sting pokes at my stomach, and I chase away the jealousy before it overwhelms me.

"He's just another client," she says, adjusting my collar. "He just wants to find a home. Help him out and then it's vacation and much needed R&R time."

She's right. I'll hand over keys and seal this puppy up and never see him again. I'll go back to fun and flings and dreams of traveling the world on my own. And he can find his girl and have lots of babies and forget all about me.

Why does what I've always wanted sound so... not me anymore?

I'm on the verge of a relapse, and I think I'll fall face-first off the wagon into his lips if our professional relationship goes on much longer.

***

We're standing outside a beaten-down mansion that—while still bigger than my house and my neighbor's combined—is completely falling apart. The previous owner's must've taken a bat to the walls when the bank foreclosed, and there are wires hanging out everywhere, a floor missing in one of the bathrooms, and the basement is about ten percent finished while the other ninety is covered in spray paint.

"Thoughts?" Cooper asks as he turns to stare back at it with an interesting look on his face.

I take in a big ol' breath and hold it, trying my best to figure out what angle he's playing from. "You still manage to surprise me."

His lips pull up in an adorable grin, and he crosses his arms. "Well, maybe you have a point about building from the ground up."

"You want to tear it down? Build on top of it?"

He shakes his head. "I was thinking more like… marrying the two ideas." He waves his arm out at the dilapidated house. "I've got the foundation, great floor plan, and sweet view. Just needs a little bit of spit shine."

"A lot a bit," I say with a laugh, but it has a weird aftertaste on my tongue, like I shouldn't be allowed to laugh with him anymore.

I can feel his gaze on me, the air between us growing thick and painful. I purse my lips together, begging my words to stay professional, my hands to keep to themselves.

"I miss you," he says, and I wish it sounded out of the blue. I wish it didn't make me miss not just him, but how he says however he feels whenever he feels it.

He lets out a breathless laugh, and I meet his gaze with a furrowed brow.

"Well, I made it twenty-seven days without letting that slip out," he says, and my heart flutters at the fact that he's counting, too.

"A record for you."

His hand twitches next to mine. "Gah, woman. Don't do that. Don't be sexy and witty or I'll get on my knees and beg you to reconsider."

"Your definition of sexy is very skewed."

He tosses his head back and growls at the sky. "There you go again."

I can't look at him anymore. I swear if I see those blue eyes and that gorgeous soul then I will crumble and fall into his arms and never leave the safety of them. I keep my eyes fixed on the house and my thoughts on how sensible I'm being, even if my body is telling me I'm anything but sensible.

"Maya…"

"Don't talk," I blurt out, slamming my eyes shut and taking a deep breath. "Don't be so forward and blunt and charming or it'll be just that much harder for me to walk away from you again." I turn to him, watch the surprise swirling around in his irises morph into dwindling self-restraint. "I'm a professional, damn it," I say, my words strong, but the power behind them that of a baby mouse. "I'm just helping you buy a house."

He steps in front of me. "True."

"Our little detour into almost a relationship will just be a fun story we tell over future dinner dates with the people we're meant to be with."

He winces like I've slapped him, but quickly shakes it off and takes another step into me. His eyes drop to my lips, and I know he wants to kiss my babbling away… and *I* want him to want that enough to do it. My fingers twitch at my sides, and my voice carries off into a whisper as I try again to convince him that I did the right thing.

"I'm only your realtor. I'm going to sell you this house

and then you won't think about me again."

His hand snakes up between us, his thumb brushing over my chin and his eyebrows pulling down. "If you think I could forget you so easily, you're crazier than I thought."

I let out a shaky breath between us. "Don't kiss me."

"Why not?"

"You know why not."

"What if I don't care?"

My lips purse together, my heart beating to the rhythm of the most romantic and heartbreaking song in history. I shake my head, unable to form words because the truth is, right now, I don't care either.

But I will. I know I will. I'll let it go too far again and then I'll have to tell the man I love that I can never ever give him what he wants. I'd have to watch his soul completely crush to dust behind those eyes that can't hide anything. I'd live every minute with him wondering, worrying over if he wished he'd fallen in love with someone else.

His warm breath washes over me, clouding my mind, turning off my brain and turning on everything else, like little electric lights snapping and popping under my skin. I move the smallest of centimeters toward him, enough of an invitation for him to take advantage of my moment of weakness. His hands slide up to my cheeks, cupping my face and cradling me in a way I hadn't realized I'd missed so much. His mouth grazes mine, I let out an involuntary moan… and my ring tone cuts through my fuzzy thoughts. I jolt away from Cooper's lips, clutching at my heart and breathlessly laughing at the heat rushing through my cheeks.

He lets out a small laugh. "Saved by the bell?"

A sigh floats off of my lips, and I reach for my phone. Holland's name flashes on the screen.

"I have to get this."

He nods and steps back, the air between us sobering me up like a bucket of ice water.

"Hey, what's going on?" I ask into the phone. Holland sniffs on the other end.

"Take me away, please? Can we just take off somewhere for at least the weekend… a week if you can. Maybe a month."

"What happened?"

"I need time away, and Warren said he'll let me go without a fight if you go with me. I'm going either way, but I'd rather not argue anymore. I'm tired of arguing."

My teeth sneak out and pull at my lip, and I glance at Cooper, knowing that time away could be just the thing for me, too.

"When do you want to go?"

"As soon as humanly possible."

"I'll pick you up tonight."

"Thank you, Maya."

I slowly bring the phone down and tap the red hang up button. There is a beat of silence before I flick my gaze up to Cooper, grateful he's given me enough space to breathe air that isn't filled with his scent.

"I have to run."

He nods. Looks back at the house. "I want to offer on it."

"How much?"

"Ten above asking price."

"I-I'll draw it up and send it over tonight."

He nods again, and we slowly head to our separate vehicles—his giant, muddy truck and my sparkly clean bug. The moment is lost in the interruption—thank heavens. I don't think I'd be able to break it off with him again, no matter how right that decision is. One time was hard enough.

25

Hide or Confide

I flop face-first onto the hotel bed, exhausted from a day and a half long drive. To my right, I hear Holland mimic the action on the other bed—well, as much as she can with the baby bump.

"My butt," she groans, her voice muffled by a pillow. "Is it still there?"

I jam a thumbs up at her even though I don't have the energy to lift my head and check for sure. I'm pretty sure her ass is just where she left it.

"You want room service?" I ask, tip-toeing my fingers over to the hotel book of over-priced food.

"Please. Then I really want to go for a massage."

"Is that allowed?"

She gives me the glare from hell, and I clap a hand over my mouth like I've uttered an f-bomb in front of my mother. One of the rules for our getaway was no questioning what's right or wrong for her pregnancy. I've failed three times now.

"Sorry, sorry," I sputter, avoiding her stare by perusing all the dinner choices. There are pregnancy massages, I'm sure, and I wonder if a masseuse could rub out a broken heart. There are a pair of them right here.

After I order us some dinner, I kick off my shoes and slide back on the pillows, building myself a comfort nest.

"You ready to talk?" I ask, and Holland doesn't move. For a second I wonder if she's fallen asleep, but then she shifts, her black curtain of hair covering most of her face as she attempts to look at me.

"I'm afraid if I talk, I'll cry." She blows her hair from her face. "And I'm really tired of crying."

Amen to that. Every time I think of Cooper I feel like I should drive to Costco and stock up on Kleenex.

"Are you and Warren going to be okay?" I bite at my lip, shifting till I'm under the covers. "Can I ask that?"

"Maybe," she says, rolling to her back. "Probably. We're just… well… *I* just need some time. Time will fix it."

I can tell she's still in no mood to talk about it, so I blow out a sigh and say, "Well, let me know if there's anything I can do."

"You're doing it."

She builds her own fort of pillows and blankets and sinks into it. "Are *you* ready to talk?"

I snort. "I don't want to cry either."

"Maybe after we eat we can get through both our drama without the crying headaches."

As terrified as I am to tell her about my visit with the doctor, I actually think it's about time that I do.

"Holland?" I start, deciding I better tell her now before I lose my nerve. She perks her head up, her brows pulled in at whatever expression I'm donning. "I didn't break up with Cooper just because I don't want a family."

The sheets rustle as she pushes herself upright. "Then why?"

Goodness, I have to keep the tears in or they won't stop. "I can't have kids."

Her small little mouth pops open, her brows up in concern as her fingers twitch against her baby belly. I swallow hard, praying that I don't let any jealousy seep into my voice as I tell her about the false positive, about the doctor visit, about the call I got a few days later confirming what they already knew.

"It's okay, though," I say when she can't find *anything* to say. "If God picked a specific number of women who would never be mothers, then it's good. I mean, it should be me. I never... I didn't want..."

But I can't finish that sentence. I can't speak it out loud anymore because it's not true. I *saw* them; for a brief moment, I saw kids in my future before that image was ripped away from me.

I bury my face into my palms, and I hear Holland move, feel the bed dip next to me and her arms wrap around my shoulders. Her baby bump presses into my side, and I feel horrible over the thoughts I had before. How I would look at her stomach and think she'd lost her mind, or she had no idea what she was getting into, or how she was going to regret that decision after the first dirty diaper. Now, all I want in the world is to be able to experience something as miraculous as carrying a child.

She holds me for a long time, her comfort only expressed through the hug and not words. I'm glad, because nothing can be said in a time like this to make it better. But her hug is doing wonders.

"What did Cooper say?" she asks, pulling back and fixing the hair she messed up while her arms were around me. "Did he... I mean, did he understand?"

I shake my head. "I didn't tell him. I couldn't."

"Maya..."

"I know. I probably should have, but he... Holland, he wants kids so badly. And he'd be such a good dad, I couldn't take that away from him. He'd stay with me out of obligation, and we'd grow old just me and him and I'd have to live with never being able to give him the life he really wanted." I shake my head, a rogue tear falling from the tip of my nose. "No, I can't do that."

"He loves you," she says, and I bring my eyes up to meet hers. "I think he'd be willing to give up kids for you, especially if you can't—"

"That's a big thing to give up. I... I am not worth it. I would never ask him to..." I drift off, tired already of the conversation, wishing I was as strong as she was with shoving away her problems. Cooper walked away; he left me because I wasn't willing to budge, and neither was he.

A knock comes at the door, and we both turn to the voice saying, "Room service." Holland pats my leg and gets up to let him in while I quickly wipe my eyes and shove everything away. Time will fix this, just like Holland said, even though so far, it's done a terrible job of it.

26

Happy Family

Tap, tap, tap.

I whine in my sleep, slapping the side of the bed. "Kat, knock it off." Little kitty is probably playing with the blinds cord again. One day I'm going to put in some nice wooden blinds so my fur babies can't destroy them.

Tap, tap.

"Seriously, Kat!" I growl, and I fling myself over. My stomach jumps straight into my throat as I topple to the floor with a thud.

"I know karate!" Holland shouts as she sits up, her arms out and her eyes covered by a fuzzy blue night mask. I rub out the pain in my elbow from where I hit the ground and stifle my laughter at the both of us.

"Sorry," I say, turning on the light as Holland slowly lifts her mask. "I thought I heard—"

Tap, tap.

A wrinkle appears above Holland's nose. "Is someone knocking?"

I stare at the door, fumbling for the remote, the only weapon in my arsenal. "Grab your phone. Have 911 at the ready."

"Maya…"

My toes creep across the run-down carpet, past the bathroom and the small closet. There's an iron in there, I think. I can use that if the remote proves useless.

"Hello?" I test, pressing my eye up to the peephole. Blond hair is all I see, the man's head dipped as he leans against the wall, his back moving up and down with what looks like labored breathing. The remote falls clean out of my hand, thudding against the floor as a gasp sucks into my throat.

"Who is it?" Holland hisses, her eyes wide, maybe a little hopeful even, but I'm too stunned to think straight.

"It's… it's my… Cooper."

She blinks fast, then her mouth splits into a grin. "Answer it."

"What?"

She chucks a pillow at me, and it somewhat jerks me out of my shock. "Open the door."

My fingers pull at the handle, but the door only gets about an inch open as the chain catches it.

"Oh!" I squeal and slam the door closed to fix it and by the time I actually get it open, my face is a ripe tomato.

Cooper's eyes meet mine, his hand slowly dropping from its place on the wall.

We don't say anything for a good ten seconds.

"How…" I start. "How did you know I was—?"

"I can't," he says on an exhale. "I can't do it, Maya. I can't be without you."

My heart stutters in my chest. "Cooper…"

"No," he says. He stands to his full height. "I'm not going to let you talk me out of it. I'm not going to let you push me away this time."

I shake my head. "Nothing's changed."

"Yes," he argues, stepping into me, stepping inside and allowing me to shut the door behind him. "*I* have. I've changed and I want whatever you want because I want *you*." His fingers grasp mine, his skin warm and rough and so familiar, like I've come home after a long day at work. "I want these hands, these arms, this smile, this heart. All of these, everything that makes up the person you are. That's where my family is."

I lose my breath… gone is it from my lungs, and my brain is somewhere in a cloud and my feet are somehow still keeping me upright. Why does he have to make it so hard? Why does he have to be the man who wears his heart there on his sleeve, profess his love only for me to have to reject him yet again.

But his eyes… they're saying everything he isn't— words that I know that will eventually fall off his lips, but they are staying inside at the moment. He really means it. He really believes that he could give up a life with a family for one without.

"Only me?" I ask, my voice a rough whisper. "You're okay with… only me in your family?"

"Well, and me, too." His lips tilt upward in his

signature half-grin, the smile line a heart-pounding indicator that he's telling me the absolute truth, and I feel a dip in my stomach, a sick taste on the back of my tongue that I, too, need to be completely honest with him.

"You really mean it?" I ask, building up the courage to say what I need to so we both know for sure. "You'd be willing to give up having children?"

He puts his hands on my cheeks, sets his forehead on mine and looks straight at me with those soulful blue eyes. "Yes."

And with one syllable, my trepidation, my worries, my every fear flies out the window and off into the night. My hands find his wrists, grasping onto him and holding on to keep steady. I take a deep breath, let it fill my lungs and let it slowly seep out. He'll understand, won't he? He understood without the entire truth.

"Cooper," I say, pulling his hands away. "I can't have kids."

"I know," he rushes out. "This isn't some trick I'm playing. I'm not just telling you I'm okay with it while secretly holding out hope for something different. If you don't want kids, I accept that."

"No." I lock on his eyes and hold them until he understands what I'm saying. "I *can't* have kids."

The realization hits him slowly, the light brightening across his expression. His lips part, but his breath is gone away, and I gulp and shake my head at the floor between us.

"I… I thought I was pregnant. I thought *we* were pregnant. But the doctor… she told me I won't ever be."

A warm hand presses against the small of my back and pulls me up against his strong, firm chest. He wraps me in a cocoon that not a single negative thought can penetrate, a place that I needed the day I found out, but I was too scared to venture into. His breath comes out in a long, sad sigh over my head, his arms a warm blanket on a cold day.

"Why didn't you tell me?"

"I didn't want you to feel obligated to stay with me," I say into the comfort of his chest. "I didn't want to be the broken woman who took away any possibility for you having children."

He coaxes my chin up, making sure that I have a good look at his face when he says, "You are not broken, Maya. Don't ever think that."

A hint of a smile plays at the corner of my lips. Can we really move forward like this? Could I really take the life he wanted away from him? I consider other options; I know there are more. Adoption, surrogacy... but it all seems like too much right now. I quickly push away from him for some much needed air.

"I'm not ready to talk options," I tell him. "I don't know if I *want* any other options. I'm thirty years old, and it feels like I'd have to fast forward the process because it takes so long for everything, and I'm not ready for that. My brain, my body, my heart..." I settle a hand on my chest, begging my tears to stay under control, but they rarely listen to me. "I saw that future you painted for us. I caught a glimpse of it that last night with you."

"When you scared the hell out of me in the pool?" he

teases, and I smile, grateful that he knows to make me laugh when I feel so low. My brain fast forwards to future moments when I hope he's still there to do it again.

"I saw it, Cooper. I saw a wedding and a house and a backyard with a swing set and kids with your blue eyes and my baby fat. I didn't only see it, I *wanted* it. I wanted everything." My shoulders slump, and I fold my arms, hoping to find the same comfort from myself that I had from him. I'm unsuccessful. "I'd hate myself forever if I took that away from you."

He shakes his head. "I see something different for us now. Something just as good, if not better."

"Don't you want to be with someone who can give you everything you want?"

He steps forward, enclosing us in a tight bubble that no one can pop. His hands find my cheeks, and his eyes hypnotize me into not moving a single muscle.

"You are *everything* I want."

I'm gone again. He's melted me into the floor, and I fly to the moon as his lips come down on mine. He pushes me against the wall, his hands soft, his mouth anxious, his pulse pounding under my fingertips. He kisses away my pain, my hesitation, my worries, and I kiss him back with everything I have.

"I still wish you would've told me," he says, breaking away to breathe. "You wouldn't have had to go through this alone."

"I've got my cats," I tease, loving that he can make me feel happy enough *to* tease in the middle of something so sad. "I'm never alone."

He wrinkles his nose at me. "Can I take you somewhere?"

I've missed his blurting almost as much as I've missed him. "Where?"

"Cabo."

"How did you...?"

"Facebook," he says, and a lightbulb pops on over my head. Now I have the answer to how he knew where I was. "Let me take you."

"When?"

"Right now."

I look over my shoulder at Holland, my cheeks warming at the fact that she's been listening to this entire exchange. Her eyes are so wide and her grin so full, put a bucket of popcorn in front of her and she'd be all set for the show we just gave her.

"I can't," I say, turning back to Cooper. "My friend needs me."

"There you go, making me fall even more in love with you." He shakes his head and plants a kiss to my knuckles. "After?"

"I suppose."

"All right, you go take care of your friend." His eyes flick over my head. "Nice to meet you by the way!" Then he leans into me as Holland and I both laugh. "Weird to have an audience when you rip your heart out and hand it over."

"I'm pretty sure you just won her over, too."

He grins and plants a kiss on my lips. "Now, take care

of her, and resist every urge you have to text me all the time or call and talk to me from dusk until dawn."

"I'll try my best."

"One more thing, because I can't keep it in."

"You never can."

He takes a deep breath and sets his hands on my waist, pulling me up against him. "This is what I'm gonna do... When you get back, I take you to Cabo for a week of beautiful love-making intertwined with sweaty, dirty screwing. I ask you a million times to be my wife while you jokingly shrug it off. We get home and I live a painfully long month alone before finally breaking down and asking you to move in. I sign on that piece of crap house with potential, and you help me plan and renovate, and we'll fight on every single decision, and you'll stop me from trying to do everything myself and hire a contractor. We get it done, you move in with your demon cats, and because I know how much you like them and we have the room, I buy you another one and you name it something with three letters. I build a swing set in the backyard, then you get someone to fix it so it's not a safety hazard, and we babysit your nieces and nephews because they love their aunt so much, and they love to drive her nuts. I wait six months to propose, and it's so romantic and amazing that you *definitely* say yes this time, because you can't resist my charm. How does that all sound to you?"

"Crazy."

"You like my crazy."

"Lucky for you."

He rests his forehead against mine. "I love you."

My eyelids close, and I bask in the sweetness of his words. He's said he's fallen for me, he's implied love, but he hasn't flat-out stated it like he does with everything else... so I know just how important this moment is, and just how much he means it. Maybe "family" can mean a million different things. That giving up one version of it doesn't mean I'm giving family up entirely. It doesn't have to be all or nothing, and I like the idea of that, and I can feel my feet rise slightly off the floor as I let myself dream of the possibilities.

"I love you, too." And because I need a million reassurances, I ask, "Are you *sure* you are okay with this?"

He squeezes me to him, chest to chest, heart to heart.

"You are my family, Maya. And I can't wait to start it."

Epilogue

From the desk of Robert Sterling, CEO

> Hey, turns out the brains
> of the place is going on
> vacation with his girl, and
> I've gotta pick up the slack
> ;) Forward all his emails to
> me, will you?
> -Robbie

I slide the Post-it across Coop's assistant's computer screen, cap my pen, and whistle my way to the parking garage. Good riddance; he's been a party pooper for weeks on end, and I told him all he needed was to get a little action to snuff out the blow of getting dumped. (It's worked for me so far.) Instead of taking my brilliant advice, he professed his love and hooked a ball and chain around his leg. If I'm as smart as I know I am, then I'd bet that he's planning to put a ring on it before they get back.

I hop into my Maserati and head over to Coop's for one last night before he jet-sets on outta here. He's got a pile and a half of papers to approve, and I'm not letting him leave me to it. I'm good at running things, talking up clients, and making the money that we're swimming in—I'm just not the one to call when that money needs to be *managed*.

Traffic isn't too bad considering it's six on a Friday. I take the main highway past a giant building that houses one of the fastest growing women's magazine's in the country. I've been dying to get some of our client's ads in there, but I gotta schmooze the editor in chief over there first. I hear she's single.

Coop is lodged up at a hotel with Maya until he gets a place of his own in her hometown. He said he finally locked down on something, but it'll take another few months to get it up to code. I'd wonder if Maya was just in it for the monetary perks if I hadn't met her. I'm an expert in spotting the gold diggers and knew Coop was safe the minute Maya picked the picture she did from the test shoot. She picked the one that Coop looked the best in, not her. She definitely had better shots—not that she had any unflattering ones— but I found it sorta interesting that she chose one that focused more on him. As much as I hate seeing my brother torn away from bachelorhood, he found someone worth giving it up for.

I drive past the garage gate and park next to Maya's VW bug. A chuckle rises from my gut from just the image of my big brother trying to squeeze into that thing.

The girl at the front desk has a gorgeous smile as I pass, and I make a mental note to talk to her on my way out. The few months in mountain city may have been successful for him when it came to dating, but it left me pretty high and dry. I'm anxious to get back on the horse now that the Cozy King deal is done and I'm back in the hustle and bustle of the city.

I take the elevator up to the top suites, slapping the thick manila folder against my palm and whistling along with the numbers as they climb and climb. The doors open to a silent hallway, and my footfalls echo around me as I make my way to room 810.

"It's *huge*, Cooper," I hear Maya's voice through the door, and I pause halfway into knocking. "How in the world did you fit that in your mouth?"

"Determination," my brother answers. "And a craving for meat."

My eyes bulge, and I rap a knuckle against the wood, holding back a smile for when I get some context around their conversation.

Maya opens the door, her mouth splitting wide when she sees me. "Hey Robbie," she says, circling her arms around my shoulders in greeting. Ain't gonna lie, that took me some getting used to. Coop and I were never a hugging type of family, but as soon as he locked Maya down for the long haul, she became extremely relaxed around me. Her eyes don't even travel to my scar anymore.

"Babe, your brother's here," she calls over her shoulder.

"Send him away! My vacation started when I left the office."

She makes a face, her nose scrunching up and her tongue slightly poking out as she waves me inside. I like her

251

more and more every time I see her.

"He's in a mood, huh?"

"Oh he's grumpy because I'm making fun of him." She brings up a maroon book, our high school name embossed on the cover. "If he didn't want to laugh, then he shouldn't have shown me this."

A chuckle rumbles in the back of my throat and I swap the paperwork Coop's gotta sign for the yearbook. "You checking out the hot dog eating contest pictures?"

"It was the only picture there was of him aside from the class pictures."

I follow her into the suite, flipping through the pages for that particular section. Coop was known for his big mouth and his math scores; high school isn't anyone's finest hour, but for him, it *especially* wasn't. I'm surprised he's letting Maya look through it at all. He must really love her.

"Did you get to the class picture yet?"

"No, she hasn't," Cooper says as he comes out of the bedroom, his eyes begging me to keep my trap shut, but he should know by now that it's my job as a younger brother to screw with him.

"He had the *worst* haircut. You gotta see this one, Maya."

"It is not as bad as your emo phase."

Maya giggles at us, sidling up to me and looking over my shoulder as she hands off the paperwork to Cooper. The moment I find his pic and slap my finger to it, she presses her lips together.

"It's okay, you can laugh," I tell her, flicking my gaze

up to Coop just in time to see him flip me the bird.

But she doesn't laugh, only lifts her puppy-dog-like eyes to my brother. "You were so cute."

"Cute?" I counter, ignoring the look of arrogance Coop is now giving me. "He looks like a Backstreet Boy."

"Don't you dare knock BSB," Maya scolds, and I shake my head. Teasing him isn't going to be easy when he's got a sexy woman here to stroke his ego. He better realize how lucky he is.

"You hold onto her," I tell him, closing the book and dropping it on the coffee table. There's a weird, heavy weight that's settling in my gut, and I run a hand over my stomach to alleviate the pressure. It's not that I'm not happy for my brother that he's found his other half. It's more like I'm reminded that things are going to be different, and I'll be honest, life gets lonely as hell when you go from being the main wheel to the third.

I gotta find myself a life outside of work.

"Oh!" Maya says suddenly, jerking me out of my thoughts. "I think my phone charger is in the bag I left in the car." A tinkle of metal reaches my ears as she stretches across the kitchen bar for the car keys. "I'll be right back."

Cooper looks up from the forms in his hands. "Coming with you."

"I'll be quick."

"It's late, and you're heading into a parking garage. It's non-negotiable."

She laughs and slips on her flip flops even though it's pretty cold out there. Coop sets the papers next to the

253

yearbook and puts his own shoes on.

"There's food in the fridge if you want," he tells me. I let out an annoyed sigh.

"I need your signature on those."

"I know, I know." He slips into his jacket. "We'll be fast."

The door clicks shut, and I slump into the couch and get comfortable. I know this whole thing with Maya is new, and his priorities are gonna be all over the place for a while, but knowing that doesn't stop me from worrying that he'll let his work go from *only* priority, to last. I can't lose my numbers guy.

I lean forward and tap the edge of the forms, eyes drifting over to the yearbook. I'm in that one, more than just my class picture, too. I got a full spread on the prom page.

Checking to make sure Maya and Coop aren't already making their way back, I reach for the book and flip through until I find the dance sections. We got a full-color yearbook that year, something that the committee was excited about. I know because one of my best friends was editor, and when she found out, she tackle hugged me in the hallway so hard I bruised.

The prom page is littered with collage pictures of horrible dancing and cheesy grins, none cheesier than the one I'm donning under my crown with Kendyl Green smiling next to me as queen. She was *the one*, at least for that year. My heart thuds thick and heavy as I remember that night, how blissfully unaware I was to someone else's feelings. Someone who meant a lot to me, too, but after that we just… we were never the same.

I flip past that page, knowing she isn't on it; she wasn't there that night—my fault—and I get to the sophomore class and stop on the Ys.

Just one picture, and I can see her in my mind as clearly as I did when we walked through those halls together. Mousey, bushy brown hair, thick-framed glasses, green and blue braces, and she always wore a pair of brightly colored hoop earrings that could double as bracelets on her thin wrists. Though I can only see her top half in the picture, I remember the lead stains between her thumb and forefinger from twisting her pencil round and round as she processed everything before writing it down. I remember her brightly colored tights and overall/rompers. I remember her toe socks, her rainbow colored backpack, her very un-cute laugh. I remember her dropping everything on a dime to help me out with a problem, hanging out on Friday nights and trying to convince her into toilet papering a house. She was probably the best friend I ever had, and I was a blind, stupid ass who didn't know any better.

I let out a long sigh, sinking back into the cushions and running the pad of my thumb over her adorable, fifteen-year-old face. She probably hasn't thought of me in years. Maybe wouldn't even recognize me if we bumped into each other, not with the jagged scar now on my face.

But if we ever do cross paths, I promise here and now that I'll do anything to get her back in my life.

To my sister,

This book is for you. I can't begin to understand what your life is like beneath the surface. I see your strength and positive attitude, your smile and the way you embrace the opportunities given to you. I admire everything about you, and I look to you as a source of comfort and wisdom when I feel as if there is nothing I can do to escape the "gifts" life has given me ;)

This book was an attempt to put myself in shoes I haven't been in before—the possibility of never bearing children. I touched the surface through the eyes of Maya, and while she found a happy ending without a miracle child, because as sad as it is, that is life, I know that it is a much deeper and more complicated feeling than that. One I will never ever fully understand.

I want you to know that whenever you teasingly say that you will have no posterity, that you will die alone, I want to reach out, wrap my arms around you, and assure you that you are never *ever* alone. I'm sorry to say that you are stuck with me. ;) Whenever you feel you don't have a family, I'm right here, attempting to take up as much room as I can in your heart. As are my children, who love their auntie so much they jump at any chance they get to spend time with her.

I love you, sweet sister. And remember next time you get frustrated with my crazy, I dedicated a book to you ;)

Love and hugs,
Cassie Mae

Acknowledgments

Thank you, reader, for sharing in Maya and Cooper's journey and for flipping to this page. (Especially if you're one of my KUs. Wahoo! Go page counts ;))

Thank you, Theresa, for hitting me over the head about a zillion times as I wrote this book. That's why you're my best friend.

Thank you, Diet Mountain Dew, for tasting much like regular Mountain Dew, but without making me go over my calorie limit for the day.

Thank you, neighbors, for being super understanding when I walked outside in loungewear because I was on a deadline and didn't have time for such trivial things… like getting dressed.

Thank you, Awesome Nerds, for reviewing this book, for supporting me always, and for sending me pictures of hot men in glasses. *Star Trek salute*

Thank you, early grays, for giving me the courage to finally go blonde.

Thank you, Beta Girls, for always having my back.

Thank you, Lenore, for sending me boob hearts on my worst days, and being genuinely excited on my best days.

Thank you, Mom, because you told me to put you in every acknowledgment page I write.

Thank you, children, for making it so easy for me to write those babysitting scenes.

And thank you, hubby, for keeping the spark alive even after twelve years of passing gas, falling asleep during date nights, and barely-there kisses as we walk out the door. That's what our family is all about ;)

Also by Cassie Mae

Young Adult

Reasons I Fell for the Funny Fat Friend
You Can't Catch Me
Friday Night Alibi
Secret Catch

YA Series

How to Date a Nerd
How to Seduce a Band Geek
How to Hook a Bookworm

King Sized Beds and Happy Trails
Beach Side Beds and Sandy Paths
Lonesome Beds and Bumpy Roads
True Love and Magic Tricks
(Buy the whole series here!)

New Adult

Switched
The Real Thing
Unexpectedly You

Adult Series

Doing It for Love
No Interest in Love
Crazy About Love

Flirty Thirty (Thank you for reading!)

Coming Soon!
Missed Kiss (TBA)
Pillowtalk (April 2017)

About Cassie Mae

Cassie Mae is the author of a dozen or so books. Some of which became popular for their quirky titles, characters, and stories. She likes writing about nerds, geeks, the awkward, the fluffy, the short, the shy, the loud, the fun.

Since publishing her bestselling debut, Reasons I Fell for the Funny Fat Friend, she's published several titles with Penguin Random House and founded CookieLynn Publishing Services. She is represented by Sharon Pelletier at Dystel and Goderich Literary Management. She has a favorite of all her book babies, but no, she won't tell you what it is. (Mainly because it changes depending on the day.)

Along with writing, Cassie likes to binge watch Once Upon A Time and The Flash. She can quote Harry Potter lines quick as a whip. And she likes kissing her hubby, but only if his facial hair is trimmed. She also likes cheesecake to a very obsessive degree.

You can stalk, talk, or send pictures of Luke Bryan to her on her Facebook page:
https://www.facebook.com/cassiemaeauthor

Made in the USA
Columbia, SC
24 August 2017